The Dark History
of the Fear Family . . .

There are many whispered rumors about the Fear family—especially about Angelica Fear. Rumors of strange powers, secret ceremonies . . . and murder.

Amy Pierce, Angelica's cousin, has heard the stories. But she does not believe them. Until she is forced to stay with Angelica during the Civil War.

On her very first night with the Fears, Amy senses something evil in their New Orleans mansion. And within days she witnesses three deaths.

Amy is terrified that she will be the next victim of Angelica's dark magic.

D1611789

Books by R. L. Stine

Fear Street
THE NEW GIRL
THE SURPRISE PARTY
THE OVERNIGHT
MISSING
THE WRONG NUMBER
THE SLEEPWALKER
HAUNTED
HALLOWEEN PARTY
THE STEPSISTER
SKI WEEKEND
THE FIRE GAME
LIGHTS OUT
THE SECRET BEDROOM
THE KNIFE
PROM QUEEN
FIRST DATE
THE BEST FRIEND
THE CHEATER
SUNBURN
THE NEW BOY
THE DARE
BAD DREAMS
DOUBLE DATE
THE THRILL CLUB
ONE EVIL SUMMER
THE MIND READER
WRONG NUMBER 2
TRUTH OR DARE
DEAD END
FINAL GRADE
SWITCHED
COLLEGE WEEKEND
THE STEPSISTER 2
WHAT HOLLY HEARD
THE FACE
SECRET ADMIRER
THE PERFECT DATE
THE CONFESSION
THE BOY NEXT DOOR

Fear Street Super Chillers
PARTY SUMMER
SILENT NIGHT
GOODNIGHT KISS
BROKEN HEARTS
SILENT NIGHT 2
THE DEAD LIFEGUARD
CHEERLEADERS: THE NEW EVIL
BAD MOONLIGHT
THE NEW YEAR'S PARTY

The Fear Street Saga
THE BETRAYAL
THE SECRET
THE BURNING

Fear Street Cheerleaders
THE FIRST EVIL
THE SECOND EVIL
THE THIRD EVIL

99 Fear Street: The House of Evil
THE FIRST HORROR
THE SECOND HORROR
THE THIRD HORROR

The Cataluna Chronicles
THE EVIL MOON
THE DARK SECRET
THE DEADLY FIRE

Fear Street Sagas
A NEW FEAR
HOUSE OF WHISPERS

Other Novels
HOW I BROKE UP WITH ERNIE
PHONE CALLS
CURTAINS
BROKEN DATE

Available from ARCHWAY Paperbacks

For orders other than by individual consumers, Pocket Books grants a discount on the purchase of **10 or more** copies of single titles for special markets or premium use. For further details, please write to the Vice-President of Special Markets, Pocket Books, 1633 Broadway, New York, NY 10019-6785, 8th Floor.

For information on how individual consumers can place orders, please write to Mail Order Department, Simon & Schuster Inc., 200 Old Tappan Road, Old Tappan, NJ 07675.

FEAR STREET SAGAS® #2
R.L. STINE

House of Whispers

A Parachute Press Book

AN ARCHWAY PAPERBACK
Published by POCKET BOOKS
New York London Toronto Sydney Tokyo Singapore

The sale of this book without its cover is unauthorized. If you purchased this book without a cover, you should be aware that it was reported to the publisher as "unsold and destroyed." Neither the author nor the publisher has received payment for the sale of this "stripped book."

This book is a work of fiction. Names, characters, places and incidents are products of the author's imagination or are used fictitiously. Any resemblance to actual events or locales or persons, living or dead, is entirely coincidental.

AN ARCHWAY PAPERBACK *Original*

An Archway Paperback published by
POCKET BOOKS, a division of Simon & Schuster Inc.
1230 Avenue of the Americas, New York, NY 10020

Copyright © 1996 by Parachute Press, Inc.

All rights reserved, including the right to reproduce
this book or portions thereof in any form whatsoever.
For information address Pocket Books, 1230 Avenue
of the Americas, New York, NY 10020

ISBN: 0-671-52953-6

First Archway Paperback printing June 1996

10 9 8 7 6 5 4 3 2 1

FEAR STREET is a registered trademark of
Parachute Press, Inc.

AN ARCHWAY PAPERBACK and colophon are registered
trademarks of Simon & Schuster Inc.

Cover art by Lisa Falkenstern

Printed in the U.S.A.

IL 7+

R. L. Stine wishes to thank
Wendy Haley
for her contributions and efforts
on this manuscript.

PART ONE

House of Whispers

Chapter
1

October 1863

What will it be like living with Angelica Fear?
Amy wondered nervously. She stared out the window as the carriage rolled past the stately homes and moss-covered trees of New Orleans. Bringing her closer and closer to the Fear family.

Amy Pierce had heard stories about Angelica. Whispered rumors that she possessed a dark and terrible power.

But Amy did not want to believe the gossip. Her father and Angelica were cousins. He always defended Angelica. He insisted that the ugly rumors had been started by people who were jealous of Angelica's beauty, wealth, and sophistication.

"Excuse me, miss," the driver said, glancing at

her over his shoulder. "It's none of my business, but are you going to the Fears'?"

He sounds nervous, Amy thought. *Has he heard the stories about the Fears?*

"My father was badly hurt in the war," Amy explained. Her voice trembled a little. "My mother has gone to Virginia to take care of him. I am to stay with the Fears until she comes home."

He looked at her again, a worried expression on his face. "Wasn't there anywhere else you could go?" he asked. "Some relative somewhere?"

"Mrs. Fear is my second cousin," Amy replied. "She is in need of a companion while her husband is away doing his war work."

"Sorry, miss," the driver said quickly. "I didn't mean anything by my questions. My missus always says I talk too much." He slapped the reins against the horses' backs, urging them to go faster.

Amy's stomach tightened. She wished she could have remained at home. She could take care of herself.

But young ladies were not allowed to stay alone. No matter how capable they were. It was not proper, her mother said.

And Cousin Angelica *does* need help, Amy reminded herself. She had two girls and three little boys to look after with no husband to help.

Secretly, Amy felt relieved Angelica's husband would not be at home. She had heard stories about Simon Fear, too. Some people thought he killed all Angelica's suitors so Angelica would be forced to marry him.

And most people agreed that Simon's "war work" involved selling supplies to whichever side would pay the highest price. Would he truly aid the North? Amy wondered. Even the Union soldiers who held New Orleans—his home—captive?

Amy leaned forward and tapped the driver's shoulder. "What can you tell me about the Fears? I met them only once, when I was a little girl. But I do not remember much."

"I cannot tell you anything about the Fears," he muttered. "Nothing at all."

"Then why are you afraid of them?" Amy asked.

"I'm not," the man shot back. "I told you. I do not know anything about them."

He is lying, Amy thought. *I know it. But why?*

With a sharp snap of the reins, the driver turned the carriage onto a long, curving drive. Amy drew in her breath as she caught sight of the Fears' mansion. It was the biggest house she had ever seen. And the most elegant. White marble columns stood in rows on both sides of the front door.

The carriage jerked to a halt in front of the broad porch steps. The driver helped her down, and dropped Amy's bag on the ground beside her. Then he jumped back into the carriage and hurriedly drove away.

A cold shiver ran up Amy's spine. She felt so alone. Did the Fears really want her to stay with them? Or did they feel it was their duty?

A beautiful dark-haired woman came out onto the porch. Angelica Fear. She was even more beautiful than Amy remembered. Her green eyes glittered as she held out her hands to Amy.

"Cousin," Angelica called. "I am so glad to see you."

Angelica's tone was cordial, and she *did* appear happy to see Amy. Amy felt herself relax.

Angelica started down the steps—and Amy could only stare. She had never seen anyone so poised and elegant. Oh, how Amy wished she could be like that!

Angelica took Amy's hands. "Welcome to New Orleans, my dear."

Without thinking, Amy pulled back. Angelica's touch was like ice.

I hope she did not notice my reaction, Amy thought. "I am sorry it is so late, Cousin Angelica," Amy said quickly. "We were delayed by a storm."

"You must be exhausted!" Angelica exclaimed. "Let's get you settled in."

Amy nodded and reached for her carpetbag. "Do not bother with that," Angelica instructed. "The servants will take care of it."

Amy flushed. She was not used to having servants. She and her parents lived simply. Amy hoped she did not appear like a silly little country mouse to her sophisticated cousin.

Angelica led Amy inside. A chandelier filled the front room with light. The floor was of pale marble, and a massive gilt-framed mirror reflected the wide staircase that curved up to the second floor.

"This is beautiful," Amy breathed. She knew she was staring, but she could not help herself.

"Why, thank you." Angelica's lips curved into a smile. "Amy, I want you to meet my daughters—Hannah and Julia." She gestured two young girls toward them.

"Welcome, Cousin Amy," Hannah said brightly. She hurried up and kissed Amy on the cheek.

"Thank you," Amy answered.

Hannah will be as beautiful as her mother someday, Amy thought. The girl was in her early teens, tall and slender. Her blond hair fell in waves down her back, and her brown eyes sparkled.

"Julia," Angelica said softly. The other girl jumped—then scurried over to Amy and kissed her. "Hello, Cousin Amy," she murmured, her eyes on the floor.

Julia reminded Amy of herself in her early teens. Shy and awkward. How hard it must be for Julia to have such a pretty sister, she thought.

Julia had Angelica's shiny black hair. But her face was plain, her jaw too wide and her nose too long.

"All right, girls," Angelica said. "You stayed up to greet your cousin. Now off to bed."

Angelica turned to Amy. "The boys have been in bed for hours. You will meet them tomorrow."

Julia obediently headed toward the stairs, but Hannah turned to her mother with an exaggerated pout.

"Please, can't I stay up a little while longer?" she begged. "I want to visit with Cousin Amy."

"Darling, you will have plenty of time to talk to

Amy tomorrow," Angelica answered. "Julia is older, and she is going upstairs now."

"Oh, Julia!" Hannah exclaimed, tossing her golden hair. "She would rather be alone in her room anyway."

Angelica laughed and kissed Hannah on the top of her head. "Hannah is like me," she explained to Amy. "She loves excitement."

Amy glanced up at Julia. The girl stood on the stairs, watching her mother and Hannah. No expression lit the girl's gray eyes. But Amy knew Julia felt hurt.

Even to a newcomer, it was obvious Angelica doted on pretty, outgoing Hannah. And ignored plain, quiet Julia.

"Off to bed now," Angelica finally said. She stroked Hannah's cheek. "Good night."

Hannah whirled and ran up the stairs past Julia. Julia slowly followed her sister. No one said good night to her.

Angelica turned and smiled at Amy. "You have grown up so!" she commented. Her green eyes flicked up and down, from Amy's shoes to the top of her head.

I must look like such a country bumpkin, Amy thought. *My shoes are too heavy, and my dress is too plain.*

"How old are you now?" Angelica asked.

"Seventeen," Amy replied.

"Such a wonderful age," Angelica said. "I see my Aunt Thelma in you. You have her chestnut hair.

And you have inherited my grandmama's hazel eyes. You are lovely."

Amy's cheeks burned again.

Angelica laughed. "I am embarrassing you." She reached out and ran one cold fingertip along Amy's cheek. "I think you are going to fit into our family beautifully," she said. "I feel as though you are one of us already."

Her words were kind, but Amy remembered how upset the carriage driver sounded when she tried to coax him into talking about the Fears.

"We had better let you get some rest." Angelica clapped her hands sharply, startling Amy.

A maid came in the door at the far end of the room. When she stepped into the light, Amy saw she had a pleasant, friendly face.

"Nellie, take Amy upstairs," Angelica said. "Help her unpack, and get her anything she needs."

"Yes, ma'am," Nellie replied.

"Good night, Amy," Angelica murmured. She leaned down and kissed Amy on the cheek. Her lips felt cool.

"This way, Miss Amy," Nellie called. Amy followed her up the stairs and down a long hall. "This is your room," Nellie said, opening a door on the left.

Amy walked in, and a shiver raced through her.

"Someone just walked over your grave," Nellie said cheerfully.

"What?" Amy exclaimed. "What did you say?"

"Oh!" Nellie gasped. "I'm sorry. It is just something my mother used to say when someone shivered like that. It does not mean anything. Please do not tell Mrs. Fear I frightened you," Nellie pleaded.

"Of course not," Amy said. "I've never heard that expression, is all." She smiled apologetically.

"You must be tired after travelling so far, miss. I will unpack your things so you can freshen up." Nellie picked up Amy's carpetbag. It looked even more faded and battered in these rich surroundings. So would her clothes.

"I would rather unpack my own things, thank you," Amy told her.

"Oh, no, miss," the maid protested, opening the worn bag. "That would not be right. Mrs. Fear told me to unpack for you, and that is exactly what I must do."

Nellie pulled a blue gown from the carpetbag and shook it out. It was Amy's best dress, and her favorite. Here in this elegant room, however, it appeared shabby.

"This is a pretty color for you," the maid said. "Blue is Miss Hannah's favorite color. It used to be Miss Julia's too, but she says she changed hers to red."

Amy let Nellie chatter away. She did not have to say anything, just smile and nod at the right times.

Since Nellie likes to talk so much, Amy thought, *maybe she will answer some questions about the Fears.*

"There," Nellie said, stepping away from the closet. Amy's three dresses and two nightgowns had not taken long to unpack. "Good night, miss."

"Don't go," Amy protested. "Stay and talk for a few more minutes. Have you been with the Fears long?"

Nellie's friendly smile faded away. "Nearly five years, miss," she answered quietly.

"Do you like them?"

Nellie shot her a glance, then dropped her gaze to the floor. But not before Amy saw fear in her eyes.

"Of course I like them," Nellie mumbled. "Please, miss, I have to go. The family eats breakfast at seven-thirty, but we can fix you something anytime."

Nellie hurried out of the room. Amy could hear her footsteps swiftly retreating down the hall. Nellie acted exactly the way the carriage driver did, Amy realized. What did they know about the Fears? What evil things had they heard?

With a sigh, Amy plopped down on the chair in front of the dressing table and started brushing her hair. *Do not let your imagination run wild,* she instructed herself. Angelica was nice to her. Everyone made Amy feel welcome.

But Amy could not get rid of the cold, chilling feeling that something was wrong in this house. "I wish . . ." she began.

The words died in her throat as a pale, round face appeared in the mirror.

It hung motionless above a cloud of white.

Dark holes for eyes. A slash for a mouth.

Amy's throat went dry. Her pulse pounded in her ears.

Slowly, the apparition reached for her.

Chapter 2

Amy jumped to her feet. The chair crashed to the floor.

"Cousin Amy?"

Amy spun around. Julia stood before her in a long, white nightgown. The face, which had been so terrifying a moment ago, became Julia's face. Amy let her breath out in a sigh of relief.

"Oh, hello, Julia," she said. Her voice shook.

"Did I scare you?" the girl asked.

"Well, yes," Amy admitted. "I didn't hear you come in."

"Mother always says I am too quiet for my own good," Julia said.

Amy's heart went out to her. Amy had been a quiet, awkward child herself. Yet she had grown out of it. Still, she would never forget how awful she felt back then.

"I was always quiet, too," Amy told her. "All I wanted to do was read books."

Julia nodded. "I like to make pottery."

"Pottery?"

"Vases and bowls, things like that. Father had a kiln built out in the garden for me."

Quiet, plain girls had to have something for themselves, Amy thought. Something special. "Do you have any of your work in the house? Will you show me?" she asked.

Julia stared at her for a moment. She appeared surprised Amy had asked. Then she shrugged. "If you would like. But be quiet or we will wake Hannah."

She turned toward the door. Amy lifted her skirts and tiptoed after her. The hallway was lit by the lamplight spilling out from the open doorway behind them. Julia's nightgown seemed to hold the light, making her look almost as if she were floating.

Julia's room was two doors down on the opposite side of the hall. "What a nice room," Amy said when she stepped inside.

"I suppose." Julia sighed. "I wanted blue. But Hannah insisted on blue for her room, so Mother picked this rose color for me." Julia lit a lamp and carried it to the large table at the far end of the room.

Amy followed. The table was crowded with pottery vases, bowls, and cups. Many were beautiful.

But some were obviously experiments that had not worked.

She picked up one of the odd-looking vases. Its ugly gray-green glaze felt strangely grainy, like a lizard's skin. Amy quickly set it aside. She hated the way it felt in her hands.

Amy studied another piece. A small bowl with a shiny glaze. "How pretty," she said. "You are very talented."

"Everybody likes the pretty ones better," Julia said.

Amy glanced at Julia and felt a rush of sympathy. Julia's face was expressionless. But Amy knew what the younger girl was thinking. "That may be true with vases and bowls," Amy said. "But not with people."

Julia shrugged. But Amy saw loneliness in the girl's eyes, and a need that Amy understood too well.

Julia needs a friend, she thought. *Everyone needs a friend.*

She set the bowl down and unhooked her silver chain bracelet. "This is a lucky bracelet," she told Julia. *It isn't really a lie,* Amy thought. *The bracelet could be lucky.* "But luck is supposed to be passed on from one friend to another, or it goes away. I would like you to have it now."

Julia stared down at the bracelet. "Are you sure?"

"I am sure. Would you like me to put it on you?"

Wordlessly, Julia held out her arm. Amy fastened

the bracelet around her wrist, then smiled at the younger girl. "There. It looks perfect on you, don't you think?"

Julia did not say anything, but her gray eyes sparkled. She ran her fingertips along the links of the chain. "Thank you, Amy."

"You're welcome. I—" A yawn caught Amy in mid-sentence. She just couldn't help it. "Oops. I think the day's journey just caught up with me. I had better get some sleep. Good night, Julia."

Amy turned away. But Julia caught her by the arm and pulled her back around.

What is wrong? She is so pale, Amy thought.

"Amy . . ." The girl hesitated for a moment. "I . . . Do not open your bedroom door at night when everyone is asleep." Amy heard Julia's voice crack. "No matter what you hear."

"What? Why not?" Amy exclaimed.

"It is not safe." Julia wrapped her arms around herself. "It is not safe."

A chill ran up Amy's spine. "I do not understand," Amy answered, trying to sound calm.

"When I was ten, I had a nightmare. I could not go back to sleep. I felt too frightened. So I decided to go look for Mother. When I stepped out into the hall, I knew something was wrong. I should have run back into my room then. But I did not."

Julia wrapped her arms more tightly around her body. Amy could see Julia's fingers digging into her flesh.

"I saw the shadows in the hall move," Julia said.

"They whirled into a black, smoky column filled with faces. Faces without eyes, faces without skin. Faces covered with oozing sores. Faces burned until they were black."

"You must have still been dreaming," Amy protested. "Such things could never exist. Never."

"It . . . they moved toward me," Julia whispered. "I could hear the faces moaning and crying. All the faces looked at me, even the ones with no eyes. Then hands burst through the column. Twisted hands, with claws. I could not run. I could not do anything but watch as they came closer and closer."

"Stop," Amy begged. "Oh, stop!"

But Julia did not. "Suddenly a man called my name, and I saw Marcus, one of the servants, standing at the other end of the hall. The column of faces rushed toward him. They enveloped him."

Julia shivered. "I do not understand why the evil thing spared my life. But it did."

Julia drew in a long, shaky breath. "The moment Marcus screamed, I raced back into my room, got into bed, and covered my ears with a pillow. But I could still hear him screaming."

Julia sighed. "In the morning, Mother and Father told me that Marcus had run away. But I knew they were lying. I found a little piece of bone where he had been standing. The column devoured him. Ate his flesh and bones. And drank his blood."

Amy felt all the tiny hairs on her arms stand up. She had never heard a more horrifying story.

Surely it was not true, Amy thought. She studied Julia's face. The girl's expression was serious. Her gray eyes held a frightened look.

"Julia, I know you believe what you saw was real," Amy said slowly. "But isn't it possible that you dreamed the whole thing? Nightmares can feel as if they are really happening."

"No!" Julia shouted. She shook her head back and forth, her black hair flying. "No," she repeated more softly.

Julia grabbed Amy's hands. "You must believe me. Promise you will never leave your room at night. Promise me."

Sweat broke out on Julia's forehead. Her eyes darted back and forth, as if she thought someone could be spying on them.

"I promise," Amy said quickly. She squeezed Julia's hands. "And you must promise not to worry about me."

Julia nodded. Amy felt relief flowing through her. Julia had been almost hysterical.

Amy gently pulled her hands away from Julia's. "I think we both need some sleep," she said. "I will see you in the morning, Julia."

Amy quickly walked to her own room—although she felt like running. *You are being silly,* she told herself. But she could not forget the terror in Julia's eyes as she told her story.

Amy changed into her nightgown. She blew the lamp out, then hurried to the bed and slid beneath the covers. Someone had sprinkled perfume on the sheets. She held the fabric to her nose for a moment. A strange scent Amy could not identify. Something spicy and exotic.

She turned onto her left side. A little moonlight filtered through the drapes. It cast inky shadows in the corners of the room.

Amy squeezed her eyes closed. The clock ticked softly on the mantel. *Tick-tock, tick-tock.* She turned onto her right side.

Then she heard another noise below the ticking of the clock. The soft sound of someone crying.

She opened her eyes and sat up. *Is that Julia crying? Or one of the little boys?*

Amy climbed out of bed and hurried over to her bedroom door. She turned the doorknob—then froze.

The crying sound turned into a low wail. And it did not sound quite *human* to Amy.

Amy could not help thinking of the smoky column Julia described. Faces whirling in the black depths. Faces crying and moaning.

"Julia?" Amy called. "Is that you? Are you all right?"

The wail grew louder. It sounded as if it were coming from directly outside Amy's door.

"Who's there?" Amy demanded, fighting to keep her voice strong and steady.

Julia's words rolled through her mind. *It ate him. Ate his flesh and bones—and drank his blood.*

What was out there? What?

Amy had to look.

She could hear her own heartbeat pounding in

her ears. Around her, the entire room seemed to hold its breath in anticipation.

Amy's hand slid on the doorknob. Her palm was wet with sweat.

She took a deep breath.

Another.

Then she flung the door open.

Chapter
3

Amy peered down the dark hall.

She studied the carpet in front of her door.

Nothing.

Amy let her breath out in a *whoosh*. Her arms and legs felt limp and powerless.

She closed the door softly and returned to bed. The odd, spicy scent on the sheets surrounded her. Amy could not sleep. What had Julia seen that night? Were the whispered stories about the Fears true? Was there something evil in this house?

Bright sunlight woke Amy the next morning. *Nellie must have come in and opened the curtains,* she thought. *And I slept right through it.*

Amy did not want Angelica to think she was accustomed to staying in bed half the morning. She jumped up, washed quickly with the water in the basin, brushed her hair, and got dressed.

She hurried out of her room and down the hall. She started to take the steps two at a time—then stopped.

Slow down, she lectured herself. Her mother would be mortified to see her racing around like a tomboy. Amy forced herself to walk down the curving marble staircase.

The first floor felt deserted. *I knew I slept too late,* Amy thought. *That awful story of Julia's is to blame. It kept me up for hours.*

Amy decided to try the door at the end of the room—the door from which Nellie had entered the night before.

Good choice, she thought when she smelled coffee. She quickly found the breakfast room.

It stood empty. But covered dishes lined a serving table. Amy peeked under the lid of one—porridge.

They must expect me to help myself, Amy thought. She filled a plate and sat down alone at the polished wooden table.

A moment later, Nellie popped her head into the room. "Good morning, miss," she called. "Did you find everything you need?"

"Yes," Amy answered. Nellie darted away before she could say another word. *Nellie must be afraid I will start asking her questions about the Fears again,* Amy thought.

Amy ate slowly. She was not sure what she should do when she finished breakfast. Would it be rude to explore the house alone? Maybe she could take a walk in the garden.

Amy took another bite of toast. The door to the breakfast room swung open, and Angelica appeared. Amy tried to smile—while keeping her lips firmly closed.

"I have a treat for you, Amy," Angelica told her. "Are you finished there?"

Amy nodded, swallowing her toast.

"Then come with me," Angelica said.

She led Amy upstairs to a room on the third floor. Thick brocade curtains blocked out most of the sunlight. A deep carpet covered the floor, and cabinets lined one entire wall. A bookcase near Amy held dozens of books.

Most appeared very old. The spines were too worn to read. Even when she could make out a word or two, she could not understand them. They were written in languages she did not know.

Amy ran her fingertip along the spine of the largest book. It felt strangely cold, and she pulled her hand away hastily.

"Do you like to read?" Angelica asked.

"Oh, yes. But we could not afford many books. . . ." Amy broke off, blushing hot with embarrassment.

Angelica smiled at her. "I am afraid these are rather . . . specialized. But we have a library downstairs that I am sure you will enjoy. Now, let's get started. Why don't you sit in that armchair by the desk?"

Amy obeyed. Angelica took the chair on the other side, facing her across the polished desktop. "You are worried about your father, aren't you, Amy?" she asked.

"Very much." Amy's throat went tight as she pictured her father in a hospital bed. She wished she knew how badly he was injured. How fast he was healing. "It takes so long for a letter to come—"

"There are faster ways," Angelica said.

Amy stared at Angelica. "Faster? I do not understand."

Angelica's gaze was intent on Amy's face. Too intent. Suddenly nervous, Amy looked away.

"Have you ever heard of the tarot?" Angelica asked. Amy shook her head. With a smile, Angelica opened one of the drawers and took out a deck of cards. She fanned them out so Amy could see the pictures on them.

They were unlike any cards Amy had ever seen. The pictures were gruesome—grinning skulls, bloody daggers, a body falling from a tower.

"They are beautiful," Amy said. *Beautiful and horrible at the same time,* she thought. "But I do not see—"

"This is the tarot." Angelica swept them back into a neat stack. "My mother gave it to me when I was about your age. Her mother gave the deck to her. It has been handed down generation after generation."

Angelica stared into Amy's eyes. "This deck of cards is very special. Very rare. It can tell us many things. Today, we will ask about your father."

"Ask about my father. . . . But it is only a deck of cards," Amy stammered.

Angelica tilted her head to one side. "There is no 'only' about these cards, Amy," she said, her voice cold. "Listen to me. They are very old and very powerful. In the hands of the right person, the tarot can show not only what was, but what is to be."

Amy felt her pulse pounding at the base of her throat. Angelica was behaving so strangely. Did she truly believe her cards could tell the future? Is that why people thought she practiced the dark arts?

"I think we will choose the Page of Swords for you," Angelica said, sliding one card out of the deck. She shuffled them expertly, then held them out to Amy. "Now take the cards. Hold them in your hand."

"I would rather not." If the cards did have power, Amy wanted nothing to do with them.

"Hold them." Angelica's voice was harsh and stern, and Amy obeyed without thinking. The cards felt strangely heavy in her hand. She did not like the way they felt beneath her fingers.

"Cut them into three piles," Angelica instructed. "Use your left hand. This reading will tell us how your father is."

Again, Amy obeyed. *Why are these cards so important?* she wondered.

Angelica gathered the piles back up. She turned over the top card and placed it on the table.

A circle, Amy thought suddenly. *She is making a circle of cards.*

Angelica turned over the second card and placed it down. Then the third. Then the fourth.

Amy knew where Angelica would position each card. Her fingers itched and burned as she watched her cousin lay out the deck.

I know how to do this. If I held the cards I would know exactly what to do.

But that cannot be, Amy told herself. She rubbed her fingers together—trying to stop them from tingling. *I had never even* heard *of the tarot before this morning.*

The tingling grew sharper. It felt like a dozen needles stabbing deep into her skin. *What is happening to me?* Amy bit the inside of her lip to keep from crying out.

Angelica turned over a final card. Pain jolted through Amy's fingers. Then it stopped.

Amy drew in a deep, shuddering breath. She started to ask Angelica what had happened to her. Then she noticed her cousin's face.

Angelica's polite smile had disappeared. Her green eyes glittered with excitement. Excitement . . . or hunger. *She is like an animal about to go in for the kill,* Amy thought.

Angelica closed her eyes and laid her hands flat on the desk. "I see a long illness for your father, and delays in his return home," she said, her voice husky. "Your mother will have to navigate through some tricky situations. But she will find help along the way, and will eventually succeed."

She opened her eyes and stared straight at Amy. "There. Don't you feel better now?"

Better? How could she feel better? What powers did the cards hold? What power made her fingers itch to touch them? What power made Angelica stare at them with such intensity?

"They are only cards," she said again, trying to convince herself more than Angelica.

"Are they? Hmmm." Angelica gathered up the cards and held them in both hands. "I think we ought to do a reading for you."

"No!" Amy exclaimed.

Angelica raised one dark eyebrow. "Why not? They are, as you said, only cards."

Angelica shuffled the cards in silence. Once. Twice. Then she held them out to Amy.

Amy clasped her hands tightly together. She had touched them once. She did not want to touch them again.

"Cut them, Amy," Angelica urged. "Think about what you want to know."

"About the future?" Amy asked.

"About *your* future. You are so young, so full of promise. What are you? What will you become? Will you find happiness or sorrow? Will you fall in love, marry? All girls wonder about these things. You, however, can know."

Amy swallowed hard. Yes, she wanted to know all those things. Anyone would. But she sensed something . . . wrong in the cards. Something dark. Maybe even dangerous. She heard whispers about the terrible price paid by those who practiced the dark arts.

Did she want to know the future? Yes. She was afraid. But something deep inside her wanted to know. Had to know.

She looked up to find Angelica watching her. Those green eyes seemed to bore right through her, as though Angelica could read her thoughts. Amy wondered again if all the eerie stories about Angelica might be true.

Then Angelica smiled, and the strange, disturbing intensity vanished from her eyes. "You do want to know, don't you, Amy?" she asked. "Be honest, now."

"Yes," Amy replied without hesitation. "I want to know."

"Then take the cards."

Slowly, Amy reached for the cards. She felt that odd heaviness again. Then the tingling sensation in her fingers. She forced herself to ignore it.

"Go ahead," Angelica whispered. "Cut them."

Amy shifted the deck to her left hand. The cards were not right. Amy knew it.

And she knew they were waiting for her to fix them. A feeling of power washed through her. Strange and exciting.

No, she thought frantically. *No. I do not want to do this.* She tried to put the cards down. But she could not. Someone—or *something*—had taken over her body.

Amy stared down at her hands in terror. They began to shuffle the deck. Quickly. Expertly.

I am not controlling my hands, Amy thought. *I cannot control them.*

Angelica's gaze turned crystal-hard. She stared at Amy as though seeing her for the first time. Amy tried to cry out, to beg Angelica to make it stop. But she could not control her voice—her own voice.

"Do not fight it," Angelica hissed. "Let it happen!"

Amy shuddered.

She felt something wrench deep inside her—almost as if a door had crashed open.

Something howled through her. Something dark and wild.

The cards flew out of Amy's hands.

She stared at them. What she saw made her shudder.

Chapter
4

The cards swirled around Amy's head. Flying through the air.

Amy did not blink. She could not tear her eyes away from the cards.

Angelica gasped.

The sharp sound freed Amy. She could move again. She jumped to her feet.

The cards fell to the floor. They hardly made a sound on the soft carpet.

Amy locked her knees to keep from falling. Her mind spun crazily. What had just happened? Had she controlled the cards? Had Angelica? Or had it been something else? Something unseen?

"It's all right," Angelica said soothingly. "You are safe, Amy. Nothing is wrong."

Amy dropped back into her chair. She stared at the other woman in confusion. "H-How can you say nothing is wrong? Didn't you see . . .?"

"I saw that you are a very lucky girl," Angelica interrupted gently. "I know you were afraid. It is only natural the first time."

"The first time?" Amy crossed her arms over her chest, hugging herself tightly. She wished she could go back to bed and pretend this was nothing but a bad dream. . . .

"Amy," Angelica said sharply.

Angelica's voice pulled Amy away from the whirl of frightened thoughts. Amy pressed her hands flat on the desk to hide their trembling. She took a deep breath.

"Good," Angelica said. "Now we can talk."

"About what?" Amy whispered.

Angelica studied her for a long moment. Then she smiled. "You are a Pierce, Amy. And there is more that binds us than sharing the same family. Some of us are . . . special."

Amy started to shake her head, but Angelica pointed to the cards. Amy could almost feel the power thrumming through her body again. Was the power evil? She did not know.

"In every generation of Pierce women, one or two are born with a special power," Angelica continued. "You have it. The cards speak to you."

"I do not . . . I never . . ." Amy covered her face with her hands. "Whatever this is, I do not want it!"

"Look at me." A hard note came into Angelica's voice. "Amy!"

Amy let her hands fall to her lap. She gazed back at her cousin. Angelica's eyes almost seemed to glow in the dim room.

"You should not be frightened of your power, Amy. It is a gift. And unless you're very, very foolish, you will come to appreciate it," Angelica explained.

Amy glanced down at the cards. They speckled the floor with color—brilliant blue, green, and gold. And red. Red exactly the hue of freshly spilled blood.

She could not believe what happened to her. *Power,* she thought. A special power. It frightened her and thrilled her at the same time.

"Try the cards again, Amy," Angelica urged. "They want you to."

They did. Amy could feel them calling to her. But she did not want to touch them. She did not like the feeling of something controlling her body.

"Pick up the cards," Angelica ordered. "When you learn to control your power, you will no longer fear it."

Amy shook her head. "I am not ready." She needed time to think. She sensed the power could be dangerous. But Angelica was right. Amy needed to learn how to tame the power. She wanted to control it—instead of it controlling her.

Angelica nodded. "I will be here when you need me. But remember, you cannot ignore this power. It is yours. All you have to do is use it."

The sound of children's laughter drifted in through the window. Amy suddenly wanted to escape out into the sunlight, where things were simple again.

"I-I think I will go outside," she said, rising to her feet. "It is such a pretty day, and I have not met the boys yet."

Angelica only smiled. Amy forced herself to walk slowly out of the room. But then she started running—and did not stop until she reached the garden.

"Amy!" Hannah called, rushing to meet her. "Do you want to play hide-and-seek?"

Hannah tugged at her hand. "Come on. The boys cannot wait to meet you."

Amy allowed herself to be tugged deeper into the garden. Past a huge bed of azaleas. Past a fish pond centered between two weeping willow trees.

Amy noticed the branches of a bushy hedge shaking as they approached. She heard a high giggle. *The boys,* she thought and smiled.

"Did you hear something, Hannah?" Amy asked. She pointed at the hedge and winked.

"No," the girl answered, her brown eyes sparkling. "Did you?"

"I heard something." Amy put her hands on her hips and turned in a slow circle. "Maybe it was a cat hiding in the hedges. Or a squirrel."

More giggles erupted from the hedge. Amy pounced. She leaned over the hedge and grabbed a small, squirming boy. "I told you it was a squirrel!"

"I am not a squirrel!" the little boy shrieked happily. "I am Joseph!"

Two other boys jumped out from behind another hedge. One looked about eleven years old. He was as blond and vivid as Hannah. The other boy was smaller with Angelica's dark hair and green eyes.

"Hello," Amy said.

"I am Robert," the older boy said. "He is Brandon."

"I am going to be nine next month," Brandon said.

"Congratulations," Amy said.

Joseph squirmed down from her arms. "Let's play!"

"Amy is 'it'!" Brandon shouted.

Catching a movement out of the corner of her eye, Amy turned to see Julia standing off to one side. The girl's expression was closed, sullen.

"Come on, Julia," Amy called. "Come play with us."

For a moment, pleasure sparkled in Julia's dark eyes. Then Hannah laughed, and the spark faded.

"Yes, Julia, come help," Hannah called. "For once, do not be an old stick."

Amy stepped between the girls. "Please, Julia?" she asked. "You can be my partner. I need help. I am sure you know every hiding place in this garden."

Julia nodded.

"So come on," Amy coaxed. After a moment's hesitation, Julia stepped forward.

"Where did you get that bracelet?" Hannah demanded.

"Amy gave it to me," Julia mumbled.

Hannah whirled around and stared at Amy, her eyes hard. For a moment she reminded Amy of Angelica.

Then Hannah smiled. "How sweet of you!" she exclaimed. "Not many people pay attention to poor Julia."

"All right, everyone," Amy called, ignoring Hannah's comment. She covered her eyes with her hands. "I am going to start counting. And you all better find good hiding places, because if you do not, we are going to get you!"

She heard Joseph squeal. Footsteps raced in all directions. Then the garden became quiet.

Amy counted to fifty, then took Julia by the hand and began the search. The girl was a bit stiff at first, but soon began to enjoy herself. Color came into her pale cheeks.

"We ought to separate," Julia said. "We will find them faster that way."

"All right," Amy agreed. "You take the east end of the garden, and I will look over by the fish pond."

As Amy made her way along the garden wall, she came across a gate. Morning glory vines twined in the wrought-iron bars, the blue flowers bright against the dark metal. Another garden lay behind the gate, and Amy could see the shape of a white house at the far end.

I wonder who lives there? she thought. With a

shrug, she turned back to the game. She scanned the bushes, the low stone wall enclosing the pond, a trellis arch heavily laced with climbing roses. So many places a child could hide.

But Amy thought the spot behind the drooping willow branches was the best. She parted the screen of branches and slipped through. It was darker under the tree. Quieter. Amy found herself holding her breath.

She rested her palm against the willow's trunk. The bark felt cool and damp, and smelled faintly of mold.

The tree rustled. Branches shifting, leaves rubbing against one another.

It sounds like whispering voices, Amy thought. She wanted to be back in the sunshine again.

Something brushed along her cheek.

She frantically batted it away. Leaves, she realized. Just leaves.

Twigs plucked at the fabric of her gown as she pushed the branches aside. She had to get out. Something was wrong.

One branch escaped from her fingers, snapping across her throat. She pulled it away hastily and felt something sticky beneath her fingers.

Warm and sticky. Blood.

Amy fought her way through the branches. Then she took a deep breath and stared back at the willow tree.

What had happened to her? Amy brushed her hand across her throat. No more blood. The cut must have been tiny.

You spooked yourself again, that is all, Amy thought. *The same way you did last night.*

Amy turned her attention back to the hide-and-seek game. "Ouch!" she heard someone cry softly. She noticed one of the rosebushes shaking.

Amy laughed. "Did you forget that rosebushes have thorns?" she called.

Amy walked toward the bushes. "I have you now." She leaned close, peering between the thorny branches.

Before she could discover who was hiding there, a woman screamed. A high, shrill scream of terror.

Chapter
5

Amy stared around wildly.

The woman screamed again.

She was in the garden next door! Amy ran toward the gate.

"Children!" she cried over her shoulder. "Run! Get help!"

Amy yanked on the gate. It did not budge. Amy pulled on it again. *Open,* she thought. *Open, open, open.*

Hinges squealed as the gate jerked open. Vines ripped away from the gate and fell on Amy.

Amy squeezed through the opening. "I am coming," she called. "Where are you?"

"Here by the arbor!" the woman cried. "Oh, please hurry!"

Amy rushed along the path, following that frightened voice. "No!" she gasped.

A woman clung to a fragile wood trellis. A water moccasin was inches from her feet.

"Run! Get help!" the woman gasped.

No time, Amy thought. The trellis began to sag.

She had to do something now! What could she use as a weapon? Amy's eyes darted frantically around the garden. She spotted a hoe propped against a nearby tree.

Perfect. Amy snatched up the hoe. She raised it high above her head and slammed it down.

The snake hissed. *Missed it,* Amy thought.

She raised the hoe again. Brought it down hard. This time the hoe almost severed the snake's head.

The snake twisted wildly. Its head flopped back and forth. Blood sprayed over Amy's shoes. The snake's fangs opened and shut near the woman's foot. Snapped and snapped and snapped.

It is going to bite her, Amy thought. She pulled up the hoe and chopped at the creature again and again.

Finally, it lay still. With a shudder, Amy tossed the hoe aside.

"Here, let me help you," Amy panted. She rushed to the woman and held up her hand. She could feel the older woman's hand shaking as she grabbed it. Or maybe her own hand was the one trembling!

"Good heavens!" the woman exclaimed in a soft, breathless voice. "I was certain I was lost. You are a

very brave young lady. My name is Claire Hathaway, and I am most grateful—"

"Mother!" The voice was deep and male.
"Mother, where are you?"

"Here, David," the woman called. "Near the
arbor."

Amy heard footsteps running along the gravel
path. A moment later a man came into sight.

A tall, lean man. His right arm was in a sling, and
a black patch covered his left eye. He had golden-
brown hair and skin that had been tanned brown
by sun and wind.

"What happened?" he demanded, staring down
at the slaughtered snake.

"It was a water moccasin," his mother answered.
"This young lady killed it before it could bite me."

The man turned to Amy. *He is not much older
than I am,* she realized. She smoothed her skirt,
conscious of every wrinkle and every grass stain
she had gotten while playing with the children. Her
hair was a mess, too.

The man reached out and took her small hand in
his large, warm one. "I am David Hathaway. Who
are you?" he asked.

"I am Mrs. Fear's cousin," she replied, her voice
a little shaky. Amy tried not to stare. But David
was so handsome. His features were chiseled. And
his eye patch gave him a dashing look.

David smiled at her, and Amy's heart started to
beat very fast. "Well, Mrs. Fear's cousin," he
teased. "Thank you."

Amy felt her cheeks get hot. She hoped David did not notice her blushing. "I am Amy Pierce. I—" she began.

"Amy!" Angelica cried.

Amy swung around. Her cousin rushed toward her, Nellie a few steps behind.

Angelica enveloped her in a swirl of silk and musky perfume. "Brandon said he heard screams," Angelica exclaimed. "What happened? Is everyone all right?"

"Yes," Mrs. Hathaway replied, pushing a lock of gray-streaked brown hair back from her forehead. "Thanks to your cousin. She saved me from a water moccasin."

Angelica's gaze drifted from Amy to the dead snake and back again. "That was brave," she said. "But how reckless! You might have been hurt."

"I would say the snake fared worse," David commented.

Angelica glanced at him. Amy could not tell whether her cousin liked David or not. But before she could figure it out, Angelica took her hand and turned her toward the gate.

"Let's get you home," Angelica said. "That was quite a scare."

"But—" Amy protested.

"And we simply must get you cleaned up," Angelica continued, as though Amy had not spoken. "You have blood on the hem of your gown. I do hope we can get it out. Good-bye, Mrs. Hathaway. Good-bye, David."

"Good-bye," Mrs. Hathaway replied. "And thank you, Amy!"

As Angelica tugged her toward the house, Amy quickly glanced over her shoulder. David's expression had turned grim. Cold. *What is he thinking about?* she wondered. *Why does he look so angry?*

As soon as they entered the Fear mansion, Angelica let go of Amy's hand. She turned to Nellie, who had silently followed them. "Nellie, take Miss Amy upstairs and help her lie down," she ordered. "She's had quite a scare."

"But I'm fine, really," Amy said.

Angelica waved off her protest with a sharp toss of her hand. "Nonsense. Run along now. I will be up later to check on you." With a swish of silk, Angelica hurried away.

Amy seethed inside. How dare Angelica treat her like this! Dragging her away from the Hathaways, then sending her to her room like a child who had eaten too many sweets. Her annoyance must have shown on her face.

"Don't be angry, Miss Amy," Nellie said. "She just gets that way sometimes. And she was worried about you, hearing those screams and all. Now come upstairs. It will do you good."

Amy shook her head. "Not unless you promise not to call me Miss Amy anymore."

"Then what do I call you?" Nellie asked.

"Amy."

"But you are . . . And I am . . ." Nellie appeared scandalized.

"Nellie, listen. We did not have servants at

home. I am not used to having someone else do everything for me. And I am surely not used to being called Miss Amy all the time."

The maid hesitated. Then she smiled. "All right, Miss . . . ah, Amy. But only when Mrs. Fear is not listening."

Amy smiled back at Nellie. She felt full of energy. "Race you!" she cried.

Amy ran for the stairs. Laughing in delight, Nellie raced after her. Amy reached her room first. She slid on the polished floor and had to grab the bedpost to keep from falling down.

"Oh, that was fun," Amy gasped.

Nellie paused for a moment to catch her breath. "Weren't you scared killing that snake?"

"I did not have time to be scared," Amy replied. "At least not much."

"Well, I hate snakes, I surely do." Nellie opened the closet and rummaged through it, pulling out stockings and stays and a billowy armful of petticoats.

"Oh, Nellie, do I need all those things?" Amy groaned.

The maid shot a glance over her shoulder. "Everything you have on is either torn or dirty, Miss . . . Amy. David Hathaway is mighty handsome, don't you think?"

Taken by surprise, Amy could not answer for a moment. Then she shrugged. "I suppose so. Really, I did not much notice." *What a liar I am,* she thought. She had not been able to stop staring at him.

"And he stared at you so hard," Nellie continued.

"Well, ah . . ." The rest of the words would not come. Amy's cheeks flamed. How she wished she did not blush so easily! And the fact that Nellie was grinning at her only made it worse. "He was saying thank you, Nellie. It did not mean anything."

"I'm sure it didn't." Abruptly, the maid's smile faded. "There is something you need to know about David Hath—"

Angelica stepped into the doorway. Nellie went very still, her eyes on the floor.

Angelica smiled, but her eyes looked as hard as green glass. "Nellie, I believe you have some chores downstairs?"

"Yes, ma'am." Nellie fled.

Angelica came farther into the room. "How are you feeling, Amy?"

"I'm fine. Remember, I am a country girl, Cousin Angelica. Snakes do not bother me."

"I am sorry that I spoke sharply to you downstairs," Angelica told her. "I was just so worried that something might have happened to you. After all, I told your mother I would take care of you."

"It's all right," Amy replied, touched that Angelica cared so much. "I understand."

"Good." Angelica's gaze drifted to the open closet. "Is that all you brought with you? Good heavens, girl! You must have packed in a terrible hurry."

Amy did not want to admit that those few gowns were all she had. So she did not say anything.

Angelica crossed to the closet and began flipping through the clothes. She made a tiny, disapproving sound deep in her throat.

"This will not do," she muttered to herself. "There are few social events with the city occupied by the yankees, of course. But this will not do at all. The Pattersons still intend to hold their Harvest Ball in less than two weeks. Lyle Patterson must have bribed General Butler himself to get permission from the Union army. You'll need an evening gown for that, and at least three more day dresses and a riding habit."

Amy sat down on the bed. This was so embarrassing! "But that is all I have."

"Ah." Angelica came to sit beside her. "The war has been hard on everyone."

"We were not rich before the war." Slowly, Amy smoothed a wrinkle out of her skirt. "But we have always made do."

"Of course," Angelica said. "And I am not saying that your own clothes are not nice. But you simply must have more to wear. I am having new dresses made for me and the girls, and I will have some made for you as well."

"I could not—"

"Amy, are you going to tell me that you do not want to go to the ball? Don't you want to dress up and put flowers in your hair and have all the young men in town beg to dance with you?"

Oh yes, Amy thought. She wanted all those things.

"Remember, dear, that we are family," Angelica

said. "We take care of each other. I am sure your mother would do the same for my girls if our situations were reversed."

"Well . . ." Amy said slowly.

"I insist," Angelica said. "I do not want to hear another word about it." She patted Amy's hand, then rose with a swish of silk. "You are a very special young lady. I want us to be good friends."

"I do, too," Amy said. But it was so hard to feel comfortable around Angelica.

Angelica started toward the door. Then she turned back. "There is one more thing, Amy. Nellie talks far too much. I do not approve of gossip. But I do think you should know the truth about David Hathaway."

"David?" Amy looked up.

"It is only natural for a pretty young woman to show an interest in eligible young men. Especially when they live next door. But you must not become attached to David. You simply must not."

"Why not?" Amy asked. Angelica was treating her like a little girl again.

"I know David is handsome. And with that patch . . . well, he is very intriguing, don't you think?"

Amy did not know how to answer.

"David used to be an amusing young man," Angelica continued without waiting for a reply. "But the war changed him. Inside more than out. Frankly, he has become a little . . . unbalanced. Some people think he is dangerous."

"Dangerous!" Amy exclaimed. "Why?"

"War is a terrible thing. Men fight for a cause. They kill and die for it. I won't repeat the rumors about how David escaped from a Union prison. They would horrify you."

How did they make David dangerous to her? Why did Angelica want her to stay away from David?

"For David, the war became something else," Angelica continued. "You see, he came to like the violence. He killed for the sheer enjoyment of it. And once a man steps over that line, he can never go back."

"No," Amy whispered. What kind of man killed for pleasure?

"I'm sorry, Amy," Angelica murmured. "But you cannot hide from the truth. David will kill again."

Chapter
6

Amy did not believe it. David could not enjoy killing.

She sat on the sun-warmed stone wall that enclosed the fish pond, trying to read. But her gaze kept drifting to the Hathaways' home. And her thoughts kept drifting back to David.

Amy could hear David's voice in her head. So warm, so sincere when he thanked her for saving his mother.

"David," Amy murmured. "What is the truth about you, David Hathaway?"

She sighed, wishing she were as smart and worldly-wise as Angelica. Then she might be able to figure out the truth.

She just could not accept the terrible things

Angelica had said. She had spoken to him for only a few moments. And she *had* seen that dark expression on his face.

But David had been in battle. He had been badly wounded. Couldn't that explain the change Angelica had noticed?

"Yoo-hoo, Amy!"

Amy turned and spotted Mrs. Hathaway standing on the other side of the wrought-iron garden gate.

"Hello, Mrs. Hathaway," she called.

"I saw you sitting there and thought I would invite you over for a cup of tea. I did not get a chance to thank you properly yesterday."

Amy glanced at the house. She knew she should ask Angelica's permission, but her cousin was very busy today. And if she asked, Angelica would say no. "I would like that," she said, rising to her feet.

Mrs. Hathaway opened the gate for Amy and led the way back to the house. She chattered all the way there. Amy found herself liking the older woman more and more.

"This way," Mrs. Hathaway said, ushering Amy into the mansion.

Amy immediately noticed a difference between this house and the Fears'. They were both huge, elegant homes. But this one was filled with furniture that had obviously been used by many generations of Hathaways.

"This reminds me of home," she said.

Mrs. Hathaway smiled at her. "How?"

"Oh, ours is very small, and not anywhere near

so elegant," Amy said. "But it feels the same. It is as if the furniture is begging to have you put your feet up on it."

How unsophisticated I must sound, Amy thought. *Why don't I think before I blurt things out?*

Mrs. Hathaway laughed. "We do put our feet on it, dear. Furniture that cannot be used and enjoyed might as well be put in the fireplace."

She showed Amy to a sitting room that was as warm and cozy as the inside of a glove. Amy settled into a fat overstuffed chair. "I will ring for our tea," Mrs. Hathaway said, tugging the bellpull.

A maid came in a moment later, pushing a silver cart. Amy's mouth began to water as she smelled fresh-baked pastries. Mrs. Hathaway poured a cup of tea for Amy and one for herself.

"Now, tell me all about—" Mrs. Hathaway began. Then her gaze moved to a spot behind Amy, and she raised her voice. "David! Where are you running off to? Come join us!"

Turning, Amy saw David standing on the stairs. He swung around slowly, almost reluctantly. Was he trying to avoid her?

David strode to the sofa and sat down beside his mother, a grim expression on his face.

"Amy has come for tea," Mrs. Hathaway said. "And Ida has made your favorite scones."

"They aren't my favorite," he muttered. "Hello, Amy."

He was angry again. Why? He was so friendly when they first met—then suddenly he changed. Amy could not understand it.

49

"Hello, David," she replied. Amy felt proud that her voice did not quiver the way her insides did.

Mrs. Hathaway handed her a cup of steaming tea. The cup and saucer were as thin and delicate as an eggshell, and painted with dogwood blossoms.

"This is beautiful china," Amy said. She tried to focus all her attention on Mrs. Hathaway. David was too unnerving.

Mrs. Hathaway beamed. "There is a wonderful story about that china, Amy. My great-grandfather brought it from France for his bride, Isabella. He adored her. He kept the box in his berth on the ship. The china survived through storms, pirate attacks, and all kinds of danger. Not one piece was broken. Only a few pieces remain today, but I do treasure them."

Amy smiled at the romantic story. She shot a quick glance at David. He shifted position slightly. *He is trying to keep me from seeing the damaged side of his face,* she realized.

So that was it! He was ashamed of his patch. That was why he appeared angry and withdrawn. He must have forgotten about it when we first met, she thought, because he was so worried about his mother.

How could people believe there was something evil in David? For a moment, her heart felt too big for her chest.

"It does not bother me." Amy clapped her hand over her mouth, horrified that she had spoken the thought aloud.

David looked as shocked as she felt. "What?"

Well, she thought, he will never speak to me again, so I might as well say everything. "The eye patch. It is not ugly. In fact, it gives you a rakish look."

Mrs. Hathaway drew her breath in sharply.

"Rakish," he repeated, his voice flat. Then David started to laugh. A deep, rich, wonderful laugh.

Amy nearly spilled her tea. "What is so funny?" she demanded. "Should I pretend that I do not see your eye patch or that sling on your arm?"

"Are you always so outspoken, Amy Pierce?" he asked.

She blushed. Not again, she thought. Am I going to blush every time I speak to him? "I was brought up in the country, where people tend to speak their minds," she explained. "Besides, a lot of men have been wounded in the war. My father—"

Her voice caught, and she took a breath before continuing. "My father is fighting for his life right now. And I do not care if he has eyes or arms or legs, as long as he comes back home."

David's gaze blazed into hers. "Is that how you feel?" he asked.

"Yes!" Of course that was how she felt. Did he think she would rather have her father dead than alive and injured?

Mrs. Hathaway cleared her throat. "Women have always been more practical than men, my son. More tea, Amy?"

Amy held out her cup to be filled. Her hand

shook as she stirred, rattling the spoon against the cup.

David leaned back, plopping his booted feet on the polished table in front of him. The tension inside Amy evaporated. She stopped worrying that they would find her unsophisticated.

Mrs. Hathaway did most of the talking—to Amy's relief. She could not seem to keep her gaze from drifting to David. He smiled at some comment his mother made, and Amy noticed that he had a dimple at the right corner of his mouth. She stared, fascinated.

Then she realized he was looking straight at her.

He caught her staring at him! She had never been more embarrassed in her life.

Amy glanced away hastily. At least he is not worried about his patch anymore, she thought.

The mantel clock chimed. Five o'clock! She had been here more than two hours. It seemed like only a few minutes.

"I should go," she said. "Angelica must be wondering what happened to me."

David rose. "I'll walk you home."

Amy turned to Mrs. Hathaway. Impulsively, she leaned down and kissed the older woman on the cheek. "I had a wonderful afternoon," she said.

"So did I." Mrs. Hathaway's eyes glowed with pleasure. "And do not forget to come back soon."

David led Amy out the back door. The weather had changed. Dark clouds piled up on the horizon, blocking out the sun. A chilly breeze tossed the tree branches and whipped dead leaves along the path.

What should she say? Without Mrs. Hathaway around, Amy felt shy and awkward.

"It is going to rain," David said.

"Soon," she added. One word. Very good, Amy, she scolded herself.

Neither spoke as they walked along the path that led to the far end of the garden. David seemed to be deep in thought. Everything Amy could think of to say sounded silly to her.

"Where is your father?" he finally asked.

"In Virginia," Amy answered, relieved that the silence had been broken. "My mother is there tending him. That is why I am staying here with my cousin."

"Would you like me to try to find out about him?" David asked.

Remembering Angelica's offer to do the same, Amy shivered. "Do you think you can?"

"I still have friends in the army," he replied. "If you can tell me what city your parents are—"

"I cannot," she said. "Mother had to move him because of the fighting."

He sighed. "That makes it more difficult. But I will do my best."

"Thank you, David."

They reached the gate. Amy started to open it, but David caught her hand and brought her around to face him.

"Now it is my turn to thank you," he said.

She looked up at him in surprise. "Why?"

"For making me stop feeling sorry for myself." He smiled at her. "At least for an afternoon."

A big, fat raindrop splashed on her nose. Before she could react, David reached out and wiped it away with his thumb. Her heart raced madly.

"You have freckles," he said.

She covered her nose with her hand. "I hate them."

"I like freckles."

Another drop came down on her head, and a third plopped onto David's shoulder, leaving a dark splash mark on the brown wool. More drops fell.

"It is getting worse," Amy said. "If you go one way and I go the other, we both might make it home without getting soaked." And Angelica will not see us together, Amy thought.

He reached past her and opened the gate. "I will see you again, Amy Pierce," he said quietly. "Soon."

Amy slipped through the gate and hurried along the path toward the Fear mansion. She gave a little skip. He wanted to see her again!

Crash!

Glass shattered above Amy.

A woman uttered a high scream of terror. Amy jerked her head up.

Something fell from the third-story window. Something big. A body!

"Help!" Amy screamed. It felt as if the word were slowly being dragged from her lips.

Nellie. It was Nellie.

Chapter
7

"**N**oooo!" Amy screamed.

Nellie clawed at the air, her mouth open in terror.

She hit the flagstones facedown. The thump sounded like a melon hitting a hardwood floor.

Amy ran to Nellie. She threw herself down next to Nellie's motionless body.

"Oh, Nellie," she whispered. "How did this happen?"

The maid whimpered.

Amy's breath went out in a gasp. Nellie still lived!

Oh, there was so much blood! Too much. It seeped from beneath Nellie's body, staining the stones red.

Gently, Amy slid her arm beneath the maid and turned her onto her back.

Nellie had no face. Only a mass of bloody flesh.

Huge patches of skin had been scraped away by the rough flagstones. Amy could see thick strands of muscle and spidery veins.

One of Nellie's eyes was shoved deep into her skull. The other had turned red with blood.

Nellie's bottom lip had been torn away completely. Her teeth were broken and jagged.

Amy saw pieces of white bone poking through Nellie's dark hair. Her skull had been split open.

Amy knew there was nothing she could do. She wanted to run away, to forget she had seen this. But she could not leave Nellie all alone. Not like this.

Amy swallowed hard. She touched Nellie gently on the shoulder. "I am here. I am right here, Nellie. I will not leave you."

Nellie opened her torn lips. Blood and bits of broken teeth welled out.

"Amy," she managed to croak. "Be . . . careful . . . of . . ."

A long, bubbling breath spewed out of her. Blood foamed from her mouth and ran onto the ground. She sagged against Amy's arm.

For a moment Amy felt very calm. She patted Nellie's shoulder again, let her breath out in a deep sigh.

Then Amy raised her hand. Blood dripped from her fingers and ran down her wrist.

Amy's body froze. Her mind stopped working.

The back door flew open. Angelica ran toward

her. She was yelling. Amy could see her mouth opening and closing. But she could hardly hear Angelica. She sounded so far away.

Someone grabbed Amy from behind and pulled her to her feet.

"Amy!" A new voice. Louder. "Amy!"

David. It was David's voice. David's strong arm around her.

Only then did she realize she was screaming. But she could not stop. Her eyes stayed locked on Nellie's mangled face. And the screams kept pouring out of Amy.

David pulled her around to face him. Amy clenched her teeth together, forcing the screams to stop.

"David, take her inside," Angelica ordered.

David urged Amy toward the house. She could hardly walk. Her legs kept shaking. When they reached the back door, Amy twisted around. She needed to get one last look at Nellie.

What was Angelica doing? Didn't she know she could not help Nellie? No one could.

Amy shuddered as she watched Angelica dab Nellie's raw, bloody face with a handkerchief. She carefully folded the blood-soaked handkerchief and slid it into her pocket.

"Do not look," David murmured. "Let's just go inside." He led her into the house and hurried her past the wide-eyed, frightened servants.

"I cannot believe this happened. Just yesterday she was in my room, laughing and gossiping. And now—" Amy sobbed, her shoulders shaking.

"Don't," David said harshly. "It will not do any good. Just try to forget—"

"Forget!" she gasped. "How could I ever forget?"

He made an impatient sound low in his throat. "Sit down," he said, pushing her toward the parlor sofa.

He told Amy to forget what had happened. But she could tell he was fighting with his own emotions. His mouth had tightened to a thin line.

David took out his handkerchief and wiped her face and hands. The fabric turned red.

Blood. Nellie's blood.

Amy's stomach lurched. She squeezed her eyes shut, waiting for the nausea to pass.

"David!" Amy opened her eyes as Hannah rushed into the room and flung herself at him. "David. What happened? Mother will not tell me."

David gently pulled her arms away from him. "They are only trying to protect you," he explained.

"No!" she cried. "Tell me what happened."

"It was Nellie," Julia said softly. Julia stood in the doorway. Her face was as white as the wall behind her, her body visibly trembling.

Amy jumped up and went to her.

"I saw her fall," Julia said, her tone flat. "She went right past my window."

"Oh, Julia." Amy took the girl's hands and drew her to the sofa. Despite the warmth in the room, Julia's hands were cold and clammy.

"Amy? Girls?" Angelica's voice came from the

hallway. A moment later she stepped into the room.

"I was frightened, Mother," Hannah sobbed, clutching the front of David's shirt.

"There, there, dear," Angelica soothed. "Everything's all right now."

Angelica's gaze flicked to Amy. "You had better go upstairs and change," Angelica said. "You will feel much better."

Amy had forgotten the blood. Nellie's blood. A sharp, bitter taste hit the back of Amy's throat. She jumped up and ran from the room.

Amy raced upstairs. But before she could open the door to her room, something stopped her. A feeling. A feeling that she should go to the top floor.

She did not know where the feeling came from. But she had to obey it. Amy turned back and climbed up the next flight of stairs.

The feeling drew her down the hall to Angelica's study.

Her feet moved almost as if they had a will of their own. *What is happening to me?*

She opened the study door—and sucked in her breath with a sharp hiss.

Broken glass hung from the window frame.

Nellie fell from *this* room.

Amy's heart pounded painfully in her chest.

She noticed a feather duster on the floor. She walked over and picked it up. "Oh, Nellie," she murmured.

Then Amy saw Angelica's cards sitting on the

desk. Without thinking, she reached for them. They felt warm in her hand. Welcoming her.

Angelica said the cards spoke to Amy. Could they have called her upstairs?

Amy shivered. Impossible, she thought. But she did not feel so sure.

Amy started to shuffle the cards. Again, she felt that strange, disturbing sensation of losing control of her own hands.

But this time she did not fight it.

She shuffled the deck expertly, as though she had done it a thousand times. Her hands knew when to stop.

The top card almost seemed to slither beneath her fingertips.

She turned it over.

The Death card.

The grinning skeleton stared at her, its eye sockets empty. The skeleton wore a knight's armor, and rode a white horse through a charred, black landscape. The only color in the picture was the red crest topping the skeleton's helmet. Red.

The same red as Nellie's blood.

Death had touched Amy today—even if it was not her own.

Was this the message the cards wanted to give her? she wondered. No. It did not feel complete.

Closing her eyes, Amy let the power direct her. She slipped the Death card back into the deck and began to shuffle again.

Again, she knew the right moment to stop. She

opened her eyes. Then she flipped the top card over.

Death.

There is nothing to be afraid of, she told herself. *The cards have just repeated the same message.*

She started to set the cards down—then found herself shuffling them again.

She knew what the top card would be. She flipped it over anyway. She had to.

Death.

The skeleton grinned at her.

"Amy?"

David's voice startled her. She dropped the cards onto the desk and spun around. Her face must have looked awful, because David strode forward and grasped her arm.

"You should not have come here," he said, glancing at the shattered window.

"I had to," she replied. "Don't worry. I am not going to faint. What are you doing up here?"

The sun gleamed on his black eye patch. "I wanted to make sure you were all right. You said you were. But I was not sure you were telling the truth."

"I think I'm fine." Amy hesitated for a moment, unsure how he would take her question. Then she plunged on. "Do you really believe a person can forget something like this? Someone dying in such a horrible way?"

His expression grew grim, almost angry. *His moods change so quickly,* Amy thought.

"I hope you can, but I never did," he replied.

Amy wrapped her arms around herself. "It happened so fast. One moment she was alive, the next . . . broken. It is like a dream. If I could just find a way to wake up, everything would be all right again."

David looked at her for a long moment. "I know," he said finally. "It was the same in the war. One moment men were fighting beside me. The next moment, they were dead."

Amy could hardly imagine facing death after death. No wonder Angelica found David changed. The war would change anyone.

But Amy could not believe he had come to enjoy killing. She could hear the pain in his voice when he talked about the men who had died.

Amy sighed. "How could Nellie have fallen from the window? How could such an accident happen?"

"It was no accident," David said harshly.

Chapter
8

It had been a week since Nellie's death. But Amy could not stop thinking about her. Every time she closed her eyes she saw Nellie's broken body.

"Do you like it?" Angelica asked.

Amy forced herself to smile, pushing the dark thoughts away. She turned in front of the mirror to admire the buttercup-yellow gown Angelica had given her. It really was the most elegant dress she had ever worn, but she still worried that she wouldn't fit in at the ball tonight.

Amy looked at her cousin's reflection in the mirror. Angelica sat on the bed, Julia and Hannah on either side of her. "I love it, Angelica. Thank you."

"I wish I were going to the Harvest Ball," Hannah said. "I would wear blue." She tossed her blond curls. "And I would dance every dance with David."

"He's too old for you," Julia muttered.

"That is quite enough, Julia," Angelica said sharply.

He's not too old for me, Amy thought. She hoped David would be at the ball.

She felt drawn to him. Despite Angelica's warnings, despite his dark moods, she wanted to see him again.

And she wanted to ask him exactly what he meant when he said Nellie's death was not an accident.

She should have asked him at the time. But she was speechless with shock for a moment—and he left before her mind started working again.

He probably meant that Nellie deliberately jumped. But Nellie wouldn't kill herself. She was too happy, too full of life.

Julia came up behind Amy. "I want you to borrow my luck," Julia said. She held out the silver bracelet.

Amy's throat tightened. Julia tried so hard to be liked. "Thank you, Julia. That is very nice of you."

Julia almost smiled.

"You would not let *me* borrow the stupid bracelet," Hannah muttered. Amy noticed Angelica did not reprimand Hannah the way she had Julia.

"Amy, why don't you sit down at the dressing table?" Angelica said. "I want to put some flowers in your hair."

Amy obeyed. She watched Angelica in the mirror as she tucked tiny yellow rosebuds into the shiny red-brown coils of her hair.

"I want some in my hair, too!" Hannah cried.

"Darling, I only have enough for Amy," Angelica replied. "But we will put them in water after the ball tonight, and you can have them tomorrow."

"But I want to look pretty tonight," the girl insisted. "I want to look as pretty as Amy!"

"You are as pretty as Amy," Angelica said. "Maybe prettier," she added with a smile.

Amy stood with Angelica, watching the elegant people who crowded the ballroom.

The room glittered. Three huge chandeliers blazed with light. The candle flames were reflected again and again in the mirror-covered walls. An arbor made of thousands and thousands of paper roses stretched behind the banquet table.

Amy swallowed hard. She fingered the silver bracelet. Would she fit in? Or would she be the only girl no one wanted to dance with?

She glanced around at the other girls, who seemed so fashionable and elegant. She felt completely out of place. Even if someone did ask her to dance, she would probably trip over her own feet.

Amy started to excuse herself so she could escape to the washroom—and then she saw David.

He was dancing with a beautiful girl. Petite with shining black hair. His injured arm did not seem to hinder him at all. Actually, he looked as if he were having a very good time.

"Well, well. There is David. And Bernice Sutherland," Angelica commented. "My, she has turned
into quite a lovely girl. David always did have an
eye for the prettiest ones."

Amy told herself she did not care. Still, she felt as
if something heavy had settled into her chest.

"Oh, Mrs. Fear!" someone called.

Amy turned to see a tall, striking blond girl
strolling up to them. She wore a silk gown the color
of the sky. It exactly matched her eyes.

"Hello, Chantal," Angelica said. "Amy, this is
Chantal Duvane, the daughter of old family
friends."

Chantal looked Amy over without speaking.
Then she turned to Angelica.

Amy felt her face flush. Chantal had obviously
decided she was not important enough to speak to.

"Did you notice that your charming neighbor
decided to come?" Chantal asked.

"Which charming neighbor?" Angelica asked.

"Why, David Hathaway, of course," the girl
replied.

"Yes, I noticed," Angelica replied. "But it seems
that Bernice noticed first."

"Oh, he will tire of Bernice after the first dance,"
Chantal said. "She is a complete ninny, and David
has always preferred spirited women."

"Well, no one has ever accused you of lacking
spirit," Angelica said with a smile.

*Angelica is not even trying to include me in the
conversation,* Amy thought. She felt more uncom-
fortable than ever standing next to this elegant girl.

Amy forced herself to smile—in case David happened to look their way.

David waltzed by with his partner. A gleam came into Chantal's eyes, a mixture of longing and jealousy that Amy understood all too well.

"David looks handsome tonight, don't you think?" Chantal asked. "That patch does not mar his looks at all. But then, good looks run in his family."

Angelica laughed. Amy had to grit her teeth. Obviously Chantal was interested in David. Very interested.

Chantal whipped her fan open. "Mrs. Fear, I know mother told you that we are planning to attend your dinner party next month."

"Yes, she did." Angelica's right brow went up a notch.

"Well . . ." The blonde hesitated, fanning herself. "I understand that the Hathaways are coming, too. I would be ever so grateful if you would seat me beside David."

"It seems David has conquered yet another heart, Amy," Angelica trilled.

She is determined to make me lose interest in David, Amy thought.

The music ended. Amy's gaze drifted to the spot where she had last seen David.

She stiffened in surprise when she saw him striding toward her. Or toward Chantal. He was probably going to ask the blonde to dance.

David reached their group and bowed a greeting.

Then he held out his hand. "May I have this dance, Amy?"

She had already started to turn away. Surprised, she swung back around. As she did, she caught sight of Angelica's face. Her green eyes had gone hard and cold, and disapproval thinned her mouth.

But Amy did not care. David had asked her, not Chantal. She felt as though she were floating.

"I would love to dance," she murmured.

Taking her hand, David led her onto the dance floor. He put his uninjured arm around her waist. "You look pretty tonight," he said.

"I . . . It is the dress," she blurted. What a stupid thing to say! Chantal probably always knew the proper response for every occasion.

"No, it is not the dress," he replied. His arm tightened around her just a little, enough to set her heart beating fast. She had never felt like this before.

Too soon, the music ended. David held onto her a moment longer than necessary, then took a step backward. It was over. Amy started to return to Angelica, but he reached out and touched her arm.

"Would you like some punch?" he asked.

She nodded happily. He tucked her hand into the crook of his arm and led her toward the banquet table.

He stopped at a row of chairs along one wall. "Wait here," he said, settling her into one of the chairs. "I will be right back."

Amy watched him continue on to the banquet

table. It held trays of ham and turkey, pastries and fancy rolls. Huge silver bowls overflowed with fruit. Silver candlesticks held tall, white candles. The flames seemed to flicker in time with the music.

The far end of the table held a crystal punch bowl. It had been cut in the shape of a swan, and floated on a bed of paper roses that matched those in the trellis.

Amy studied the huge arching trellis behind the long table. She tried to imagine how many people had worked to make all those blossoms out of paper and wire. It was amazing.

She glanced away in time to see Bernice Sutherland wrap her arm around David and lead him into the narrow space between the trellis and the wall. It does not matter, Amy told herself.

But it did. He had forgotten her. How could she think that David would prefer her over these beautiful, sophisticated girls?

Tears blurred her vision, turning the candlelight into a golden haze.

Amy brushed the wetness from her eyes. But the flickering bright haze did not go away. It grew stronger.

"Fire!" someone cried.

The musicians stopped abruptly.

A woman screamed. People rushed for the doors. Shoving and pushing. Overturning chairs and tables. Plates and glasses shattering on the floor.

Amy could not move. Not until she knew David

was safe. She ran toward the spot where he and Bernice had disappeared, fighting her way against the crowd.

She could see the long banquet table. Behind it, fire licked hungrily at the trellis. As she watched, flames leaped to the curtains, jumping from window to window.

"David!" she cried. "Where are you?" Amy pushed her way closer. She had to find him.

Flames exploded through the paper blossoms of the trellis. Sparks and black ash sprayed everywhere.

Amy staggered back. She raised her arm to shield her face and hair from the cascading sparks.

Then someone burst through the burning trellis. A woman. Bernice Sutherland. She uttered a long howl of agony.

The back of Bernice's gown was on fire. Flames raced through the silk fabric. Too fast. In an eyeblink, her whole dress was burning.

And then her hair caught fire.

Shrieking, Bernice beat at the flames as she ran. Amy tried to catch her. But Bernice spun away, still screaming.

Amy snatched up a tablecloth and raced after her.

Flames poured from Bernice's clothes, her hair. Blackened shreds of cloth peeled away from her and fell smoking on the floor. She screamed again and again, loud and high.

"Bernice, stop!" Amy cried. "Do not run."

Bernice turned to face her.

Amy gasped.

Bernice's skin bubbled like wax that was just starting to boil. Some of it fell away from her every time she screamed. Her hair clung to her scalp in sizzling clumps.

Then her skin turned the color of charcoal, blackening like meat cooked too long on a spit. She looked like a doll, a flaming scarecrow, anything but a human being.

Amy threw the tablecloth over the burning girl and smothered the flames.

Bernice fell to the floor. Smoke oozed out from beneath the cloth. Smoke that reeked of burnt hair, and cloth, and flesh.

Bernice's screams stopped suddenly. She was out of pain now, Amy told herself. At least she was out of pain.

Sparks rained down all around Amy. She looked up. The huge trellis swayed back and forth.

The wood groaned like an animal in pain.

There was no time to run. Amy flung her arms up as the flaming trellis fell straight toward her.

Chapter 9

The banquet table tipped over with a *crash!*

Amy felt heat blasting across her face.

Then she flew off her feet backwards.

She landed with a jolt that drove the breath out of her lungs. Something hard landed on top of her.

The world shattered into black spots.

Then Amy's vision cleared and she found herself sprawled on the floor. David lay half on top of her.

"Are you all right?" he panted.

Amy coughed, the smoke choking her. "David . . . you saved me."

He got to his feet, and hauled her up beside him. "The next time I tell you to wait, I expect you to do what I say!" he snapped.

Before she could say anything, David grabbed

her shoulders and turned her toward the closest door. "Get out of here," he growled.

"But what about you?"

"I will be fine." He gave her a shove. "Now go! Before you end up like Bernice."

That got her moving. She wasn't sure if she ran from him or from the fire. Amy shot one last look over her shoulder. But David had disappeared.

Amy stumbled past Bernice's body. A cloud of smoke hovered above it. Darker than the rest of the smoke. Darker and thicker. Oozing over every inch of the cloth covering Bernice.

Despite the heat of the fire, something cold clawed its way up Amy's spine.

Go. Just go, she ordered herself. She dashed outside, coughing and choking.

The air felt sticky, thick with the promise of rain. After the smoke inside, it smelled like heaven. Amy drew a breath.

"Amy!" Angelica called.

She turned to see Angelica walking toward her. Their gazes met. Through the crowd, Amy thought she saw tiny flames leaping in Angelica's eyes.

A deep, cold shiver raced up her back.

Then, as suddenly as it had happened, the illusion faded. Angelica's eyes appeared normal again. Amy let her breath out in a sigh of relief.

"Amy, dear," Angelica murmured, taking both Amy's hands in hers. "We were so worried about you!"

"Bernice is dead," Amy whispered. "She was on fire, and now she is dead."

Amy wrapped her arms around herself, trying to stop shaking. "I want to go home."

Angelica squeezed her hands. "Then I shall take you home."

Amy shook her head. She did not want to go back to the Fears' mansion. She wanted to go *home.* Home to Maurepas. Home to her mother and father.

But she could not. She was trapped here.

Amy curled up beneath the covers. But she was afraid to go to sleep. She knew her dreams would be full of death.

Two people had died in front of her eyes— Bernice and Nellie. She wished it had never happened. She wished she could forget. She wished . . .

A sudden thought made her sit up straight in bed. Two people had died. Angelica's cards had tried to tell her there would be more death after Nellie's, but Amy had not understood.

Amy felt her heartbeat pound in her throat. She had turned the Death card up *three* times. Someone else was going to die. There had to be one more.

Amy shuddered. Who would be next?

This had to be a bad dream. A terrible nightmare. Any minute now she would wake up in her bed at home and everything would be all right.

But she was already awake. And she was not at home.

Click, click, click.

Something tapped at her window. Who was out there?

Amy flung off the covers and scurried to the window. She peered through the curtains.

David stood in the garden below. He beckoned for her to come down.

What did he want? Amy grabbed her dressing gown and put it on. Quietly, she slipped out of her room and headed downstairs.

She held her breath at every creak of the floorboards. Angelica would be furious if she caught Amy sneaking out to see David.

David waited for her at the back door. He took her hand and pulled her deeper into the garden—where they could not be seen from the house.

"I'm sorry I was so rough on you tonight. I just had to get you out of the fire as quickly as possible. I wanted to make sure you were all right," he explained.

"I am all right," she replied. "Other than being afraid to sleep. Afraid to dream, really."

"I know about bad dreams." David turned his head, and the moonlight glinted on his black eye patch. "There are lots of things I do not want to dream about."

"From the war?" she asked.

He nodded. His mouth tightened, and the lines in his forehead deepened.

Amy began to shake again. It embarrassed her. She clasped her hands tightly together so David would not notice. But he did. She had the feeling he saw more with one eye than most men did with two.

He reached toward her, then let his arm fall back to his side. "I am sorry you had to see such a horrible thing," he said.

"It was my first ball." She crossed her arms over her chest. "And I do not think I want to go to another one—ever."

This time, David did not hesitate. He slid his arm around her waist and pulled her against his side. Amy heaved a sigh as his warmth seeped into her.

"How did it happen?" she asked.

"Bernice wanted to talk to me," he replied. "In private. She said it was very important. So we went on the other side of the trellis, where we could be alone."

"I know. I saw you." Amy remembered how she had felt watching him with the other girl.

"I planned to come right back," he reassured her. "The moment we were out of earshot, Bernice began complaining because I danced with you. I told her it was none of her business, and started to walk away. She grabbed for me."

David hesitated. "I don't know exactly what happened next. I turned away. Then I heard a whooshing sound. When I turned back, the trellis was on fire."

A muscle jumped in David's jaw. "It happened so fast. One second, everything was fine. The next . . . Bernice was on fire."

Poor David, Amy thought. He had already been through so much—and now this.

"I could feel the heat pouring from her. Her eyes grew wide, as though she were surprised. Then she started to scream. I grabbed for her, Amy. I might have been able to help her, right then at the beginning. But she ran."

"David—" Amy wanted to tell him that she knew it was not his fault. But he rushed on.

"Everything she touched started to burn," he continued. "I thought I knew every terrible way to die. But I did not. Bernice's death was the worst I've ever seen."

Amy put her arms around him. She hung on tight.

His breath went out in a long, shuddering sigh. "Amy," he murmured, his voice low and intense.

He pulled his head back and stared down at her. Then he kissed her. His lips felt warm and hard.

Amy pulled back, staring at him in shock. Her heart leaped inside her.

"I have to leave New Orleans for a couple of days," he told her. "But I want to see you as soon as I get back."

"Angelica will not—"

"I know."

"Meet me here by the fish pond, day after tomorrow," he said. "At this same time."

"Yes," she promised. "I will be here."

He smiled at her, a slightly crooked grin that set her heart racing even faster. And in that moment, Amy knew she loved him.

He kissed her again. Then he stepped away, holding her at arm's length. "Be careful, Amy. Strange things are happening, and they are too close to you. Do not trust anyone."

"But I trust you," she protested.

"No," he said sharply. He gave her a little shake. "You cannot trust anyone—especially not me."

PART TWO

———

House of Death

Chapter
10

Amy sat on the low wall enclosing the fish pond. The moon was a thin crescent in the black-velvet sky. Shadows lay thick in the garden, and only a faint breeze stirred the leaves.

Amy drew her hand through the quiet water, shattering the reflected stars. She wanted to see David so badly that it seemed as though the whole world had stopped moving. The last two days passed much, much too slowly.

"David," she whispered.

He told her not to trust him. But Amy knew he wanted her to believe in him despite his words. Otherwise why would he ask her to meet him? Why would he kiss her so passionately?

The night was perfect, and soon David would be with her. If she trusted him, Amy knew she could help him trust himself again.

A half hour passed. Then another. Still David did not come. Amy grew restless. What was keeping him? He had not forgotten, had he?

"Amy?" a voice whispered.

Amy jerked her head toward the sound. "Who's there?" she demanded.

Julia stepped out of the shadows, dressed only in a white nightgown. Her bare feet were damp from the dew-studded grass.

"What are you doing out here, Julia?" Amy asked.

"I saw you from my window," the girl answered. "What are *you* doing out here so late?"

"I am just enjoying the night air," Amy answered.

Julia crossed her arms. "You are waiting for David, aren't you?"

"I, ah . . ."

"Mother says you should stay away from him," Julia said.

"Well, I think she is wrong," Amy retorted, angry that Angelica had made such a decision for her. "He is gentle and kind, and he saved my life."

Light flashed on Julia's silver bracelet as she twisted it around and around on her wrist. "Mrs. Hathaway came to the house today, asking for you," she said finally.

"She did?" Amy asked in surprise.

Julia nodded. "And yesterday, too. Mother told her you were very upset by what happened at the ball, and could not see anyone."

"She has no right to do that." Amy jumped to her feet, outraged. "It is my life, and I will be friends with whomever I want!" Amy snapped.

Then, seeing the distress on Julia's face, she softened her tone. "I know it is not your fault."

Julia nodded. "You are my friend, Amy. Don't worry. I will not tell Mother about your meeting with David. But be careful around Hannah. She loves to tattle. She loves to get people in trouble."

Julia took the bracelet off and held it out to Amy. "I think you might need some luck again."

"Thank you, Julia." Amy gave her a slightly shaky smile. "But I am already lucky. I have you as a friend, don't I? Now, hurry back to bed."

Julia smiled and glided silently toward the house. Her nightgown seemed to float around her.

Amy settled back onto the wall. But hot anger still ran through her. True, her mother had asked Angelica to take care of Amy. But Angelica was going too far.

"Where are you, David?" she whispered.

Time dragged on. She ought to go in. But she stayed, hoping he would come. He would not forget. He could not forget.

Amy remembered how angry he seemed when he told her not to trust him. Could he have decided not to see her again?

A sudden breeze spun across the pond, blurring

the moon's image. When the water was smooth again, the moon's image had changed. The moon had become a woman's face. The stars swirled into a pale coil of hair around her.

Amy stared into the water. She shook her head slowly back and forth. "No," she whispered.

She closed her eyes tightly. Then opened them. But she still saw the woman's face reflected in the water.

I know her, Amy realized. It is Chantal Duvane. Pale, lovely. Her mouth curved in a smile.

Then the smile on Chantal's face faded. Her eyes grew wide. Her face went slack with terror.

Chantal was drowning.

How can this be? Amy thought wildly. *Why am I seeing this?*

Bubbles streamed from Chantal's nose and mouth. She reached up, scrabbling wildly at the surface of the water.

Amy had to do something, anything. She plunged her hands into the water. But her hands passed straight through Chantal, shattering her image.

As Amy pulled her hands out of the water, Chantal's image reappeared. Amy's breath let out in a gasp of sheer horror. Chantal was still drowning. Slowly, so slowly.

Help me! Chantal screamed silently, staring straight into Amy's eyes.

Can she see me? Amy thought wildly. *Is this real?*

Suddenly, David appeared in the water behind Chantal. His hands clamped onto Chantal's shoulders so hard that Amy could see his muscles bunching.

"Help her," Amy whispered. "David, help her."

Chantal glanced over her shoulder, and hope gleamed in her eyes. Then David began to pull Chantal down. Down into the dark, swirling water.

Chantal's eyes grew so wide that white showed all around the irises. Her mouth opened in a shriek.

No sound escaped. No one could hear her.

David dragged Chantal down. Down, down, down.

Amy leaned over the water, watching. Watching. Her beating heart thundered in her ears.

Chantal screamed in awful silence. Then she disappeared into the cold, dark depths of the water.

She is drowned! Amy thought. *David drowned Chantal!*

"No," Amy whispered. "It cannot be true!"

She peered down into the water. But there were no more images in the pond. The water was solid black.

The next day, Amy, Angelica, and the children were picnicking on the shore of Lake Pontchartrain. Humidity hung heavily in the air as the sun burned away the moisture from the day before.

"Let's go play!" Robert shouted as soon as the carriage rolled to a stop.

"Let's play war," Brandon suggested. "You can be Grant, and I will be Jeb Stuart."

"I do not want to be a Yankee," Robert complained.

Angelica laughed. "Go on, children. But stay where Amy can see you and don't go near the water."

Amy swept little Joseph into her arms and followed the other children as they ran across the field. The boys were still arguing over who was going to be the Yankee general. Finally, they agreed to all be Rebels. Julia played a nurse, and Hannah a brave lady spy.

With a sigh, Amy sat down on a fallen log to watch. She had not slept much the night before. She had tossed and turned, wondering why David had not come.

And why she had that horrible vision. She had never experienced anything like it.

The image of Chantal's screaming face sprang into Amy's mind.

Stop! she ordered herself. *Don't think about it again. You love David. You know he is a good person. Nothing else matters.*

"Amy, watch me!" Joseph called.

As Amy turned, she caught sight of something white floating near the shore. It looked like a mound of cloth. Then she saw something stretching out from the pile.

Something that looked like an arm.

It could not be. Not here. The lake was blue and placid in the sunlight. Birds swooped overhead, calling to one another. Tree branches swayed gently in the breeze.

The mound had to be exactly what she first thought—a pile of cloth. A branch must have gotten caught in it somehow, and at a distance it looked like a human arm.

"That must be it," she said. "It is only a branch." She returned her attention to the children.

But the skin at the back of her neck crawled, as though something cold touched her there. She had to know. She had to be certain.

Her heart pounding, Amy walked toward the lake. She stared into the water.

Her stomach clenched.

No, she thought. *No, no, no.*

Chantal. It was Chantal.

Amy remembered Chantal's beauty. Her confident smile.

But Chantal was no longer smiling.

And she was no longer beautiful.

She was dead. Drowned.

Fish had eaten her eyes.

Chapter
11

Amy's heartbeat roared in her head as she stared at the bloody pits of Chantal's eye sockets. The fish had eaten away part of her nose too. And most of her lips.

Green moss had begun to grow on Chantal's bloated tongue.

She drowned. Just like in my vision, Amy thought.

"Amy!" Julia called. "What are you doing?"

"Do not come over here," she shouted over her shoulder. "Run and tell your mother I need her. And stay back, all of you."

They must have heard the horror in her voice, for even Hannah obeyed without arguing. Amy could hear them calling out to their mother as they ran.

A moment later, Angelica joined her. "Amy, what on earth . . ." Angelica began. Then her eyes widened. "Oh, my goodness."

"It is Chantal Duvane," Amy said quietly.

Again Amy saw David holding Chantal under the water. Saw Chantal silently screaming for help.

"Amy, keep the children away while I tend to poor Chantal," Angelica instructed.

Amy nodded, trying to force the terrifying vision from her mind.

She turned and held her arms out wide, shooing the children ahead of her like a flock of chickens. "Come on," she urged. "There is nothing to see here. Let's go find out what your mother brought to eat." The children ran on ahead of her.

Amy was sure she would never eat again. Chantal's eyes . . .

Amy took a deep breath and glanced over her shoulder at Angelica.

Wait. What was Angelica doing?

Amy swallowed hard. Angelica was bent over Chantal's body—poking her handkerchief into Chantal's bloody eye sockets. Amy watched as Angelica carefully folded the handkerchief and slid it into the bodice of her dress.

Amy quickly turned and followed after the children. She did not want Angelica to know she had seen.

She did the same thing to Nellie, Amy remembered. The same thing. She wiped blood off Nellie's face—and saved it.

How could she? And why? *Did* Angelica practice the dark arts? Did she use the blood to increase her powers somehow?

Or maybe, Amy thought, death itself fed her power.

Maybe . . . maybe Angelica killed Chantal.

But what about Amy's vision? In her vision, Angelica had not killed Chantal. No, in her vision, David was the murderer.

Had Amy's mind somehow connected with Chantal's as she drowned?

Could David have . . .

A cold, hard lump formed in Amy's stomach.

David had not come last night. Where had he been? Who was he with? And why, *why* hadn't he kept his promise to meet her?

Then came the worst, the very worst thought of all.

Three women died—Nellie, Bernice, and Chantal. And David knew all of them.

Nellie had tried to tell Amy something about him. Bernice had been with him right before she died. Chantal had wanted David's attention.

"Oh, David," Amy whispered.

Could David be a killer? Could Amy have misjudged him so? From the first moment Amy saw him, she was drawn to him. Memories flashed through her mind—David's concern for his mother, his kindness to Amy the day Nellie died, his warm smile when they danced together.

Amy could not have been so wrong about him. Could she?

Darker memories flooded Amy's mind—Angelica's warning that David enjoyed killing, David angrily telling Amy not to trust him. And her vision. Her horrible vision.

I won't believe it. I won't, Amy thought.

But nothing else made sense.

Amy felt hot tears run down her cheeks.

Her vision was still so clear. She could see David holding Chantal under the water. Until she was dead.

No, nothing else made sense.

David had to be the killer.

That night, Amy waited until everyone had gone to bed. Then she slipped out of her room. She had to ask Angelica's cards what would happen next.

She had to know if there was more death to come.

Amy's slippers made no sound on the oak stairs as she climbed to the third floor. The banister felt cool beneath her hand. What would the cards tell her tonight?

A sudden chill prickled along her spine. The hair at the back of her neck stood on end.

Someone was watching her. Angelica?

She searched the dark staircase, but saw nothing. Her heart started thumping as she remembered Julia's terrible story about the smoky column of faces. It had caught Marcus, and it had eaten him. Flesh and blood and bones.

"It was just a story," she whispered.

But was it? So many strange things happened here in the Fear mansion. Things she would not have believed possible a month ago. She held her breath, listening.

Was that smoke-thing stalking her now, sliding up the stairs?

She ran the rest of the way up the stairs and into Angelica's study. She closed the door behind her. Safe! She pressed her ear to the door, but there was only silence.

She let her breath out in a sigh. It was her imagination after all.

No light came in the window. Rain began to mist the glass. But even in the darkness, Amy could sense the cards. Feel them calling to her. *Come to us,* the cards seemed to say.

Amy took a step forward. Cold wrapped around her. A wave of gooseflesh ran up her arms and down her back.

She took another step. Ice seemed to pierce her flesh, straight through to her bones.

This is not natural cold, she thought. Something, some . . . force did not want her to reach the cards.

"I have to know what will happen next," she whispered. "I have to!" She took another step.

So cold. Icy cold. She struggled to keep going. If she stopped, she did not think she could start moving again.

Slowly, she took another step. Then another. Her feet felt like dead lumps.

She paused, gasping for breath. When she tried to lift her foot again, her body would not obey.

She tried to cry out. But the cold froze her voice in her throat.

She could not move. She could not move at all.

Chapter
12

A freezing wind howled through Amy's ears. The high pitch blocked out all other sounds.

Amy's eyelids grew heavy. She struggled to keep them from drifting downward.

Her heart seemed to be beating slower. She found herself waiting for each beat. Afraid that it would not come.

Her thoughts turned heavy and slow.

But a tiny ember still burned deep inside her. She closed all the strength she still had around it, protecting it from the cold. If that small, precious spark went out, she knew she would be lost.

She had to move. She had to fight. But how could she fight something she could not see?

"The power is yours," Angelica had said. *"All you have to do is use it."*

She had to use it now. Or die.

She focused all her attention on that small, glowing ember inside her. The cards called to her, even through the awful cold. If she could only reach them, she had a chance.

Oh, but she was cold, so cold. She did not think she could make her body obey her again.

She had to try. Either that, or give up and allow the cold to take her completely.

"I . . . will . . . not . . . give . . . up!" she gasped.

Summoning every last bit of energy she had, she forced her legs to move. One step. Then another. She staggered, out of control, reeling toward the desk.

Closer, closer . . . she could almost touch it.

Her breath felt like a solid chunk of ice in her chest.

Her legs stopped working. The paralysis seeped upward toward her heart. A moment more, and it would all be over.

Amy lunged forward. Throwing herself toward the desk. Her hands hit the edge. Gripping the desk hard as she could, she pulled herself closer.

She flung one arm across the desk. Her outstretched hand touched the deck of cards.

Heat flowed into her from the cards. The stiffness drained from her limbs. She was going to live. Triumph ran quick and hot through her veins.

The cold swirled around her. It wanted her back, she knew.

Amy closed her eyes. She concentrated on the heat flowing through her body. The cards pulsed in her hands. The eerie cold retreated, flowing away like ice from a flame.

Amy sagged into Angelica's chair. Her arms and legs shook with relief. Death had been close, so close.

But she won. She used the power, and won. She defeated whatever force had caused that awful cold. She beat it.

The cards throbbed in her hand, reminding her of her purpose. She had to know if there would be more killing . . . if David would take another victim.

"It is time," she murmured.

The rain grew heavier, pounding at the windows. A far-off flash of lightning flickered across the sky.

Amy lit the lamp and set it on the desk. She picked up the cards and began to shuffle. She was not frightened of them anymore. They had helped her. Their power had become her power.

This was the power Angelica wanted for her. All Amy had to do was learn to use it. Her way. Not Angelica's way—hers.

She finished shuffling. The cards almost seemed to move on their own as she cut them.

"Tell me the future," Amy whispered. "Three deaths have occurred. Will there be more?" She laid the cards out in a new pattern, her hands moving quickly and precisely.

One of the cards immediately caught her attention. The card had a deep blue background. It pictured a blond woman sitting on a tall throne. She held a staff in one hand, a sunflower in the other. A black cat sat at her feet.

Amy ran her fingertip along the card's smooth surface. There was something familiar about the woman . . .

Amy stiffened. The woman looked like Chantal.

The card blurred, the picture fading into the deep blue of the background.

Then the blue surface rippled.

It looked like . . . water.

Amy blinked, but the illusion stayed.

The blue widened and deepened, and Amy realized that she was gazing at the fish pond.

She felt herself floating toward it.

No! No! She did not want to go there.

But she had somehow become lighter than air. Helpless to fight the wind that pushed her onward.

She knew how this vision would end—in death. There was no escape.

Amy floated above the pond, several inches away from the surface. Chantal smiled at her from beneath the water. Amy tried to call out a warning, but her voice made no sound.

Chantal's smile faded. Her eyes grew wide with terror. And she began to drown.

Amy reached for her. She knew she could not save Chantal, but she had to try. Amy's hand brushed the surface of the water.

Amy could feel Chantal's fear inside her own

body. Somehow, she and Chantal were linked together the moment Amy touched the water. Amy could feel everything Chantal felt.

The water dragged at her heavy skirts, keeping her from reaching safety. Terror sent jagged red patches floating across her vision. Her lungs burned. She needed to breathe. But she could not.

There was water all around her. If she took a breath, water would fill her lungs.

Agony shot through her chest. Her lungs screamed for air. Air. She needed air. She had to take a breath.

Amy fought the pain. She reached down and caught Chantal's hands. She struggled to pull Chantal to the surface.

Amy felt her muscles tear. Any moment her arms would rip away from their sockets.

But Amy did not let go. If only she could stop this awful vision somehow. If only she could drag Chantal to the surface and make her live again . . .

A shadowy figure swam up from the depths of the water. A man. He clamped his hands on Chantal's shoulders. His fingers digging into her flesh.

David. It was David.

David tore Chantal away from Amy. Dragged her beneath the water.

Bubbles streamed from Chantal's mouth and nose. Her face contorted. She began to die.

And in the water below, the fish waited.

They would go for the soft parts first.

Amy tore her gaze away. And found herself

staring straight into Chantal's despairing eyes. She knew, too. She knew who the fish were waiting for. What they would do.

Her mouth opened in awful, soundless screams. Dying screams.

Everything went black. *I am dying,* Amy thought. *I am dying with Chantal.*

Then the connection between Chantal and Amy broke.

Amy could see clearly again. She drew in a deep breath. She was alive.

But something was still happening in the fish pond. Chantal's face was changing.

Chantal's features shifted and flowed, as though the flesh had turned liquid. Lines appeared on her forehead and around her mouth. Her blond hair turned to brown streaked with gray.

"No," Amy gasped. "Please no."

The face in the pond had become Mrs. Hathaway's. Would Mrs. Hathaway be the next to die? Was that what this horrible vision meant?

The older woman reached out to Amy. Begging for help. Begging to live.

Mrs. Hathaway screamed those same terrible, silent screams.

Then David swam up behind her and grabbed her. He dragged her down into the water. Down, down, down.

Down to the fish.

Chapter
13

"David, stop!" Amy cried, jumping to her feet.

The image shattered.

Amy stared down at the cards. Her entire body trembled. She knew the truth now. She knew the truth. She knew what the future held.

Mrs. Hathaway would be the next to die.

It was going to happen soon. Tonight. Now.

And David was going to kill her.

Amy ran from the room. Her slippers rasped on the oak floor as she dashed down the stairs and out the front door.

The rain soaked her hair, her dressing gown. Lightning flashed, followed by thunder that almost shook the ground.

Amy ignored it. Nothing was going to stop her from getting to Mrs. Hathaway.

"Please," she panted. "Please do not let me be too late. I cannot be too late this time."

She jumped over a fallen branch, sending up a spray of water. She could see the Hathaway mansion now. There was no light in any of the windows.

What would she find there? Would she be in time to save Mrs. Hathaway?

Amy forced herself to run faster. She slipped as she ran up the steps to the mansion, skidding painfully on her knees.

But she was up a moment later. She had to be in time. She had to.

The door was unlocked. Amy flung it open and rushed inside. Lightning flared across the sky. Searing white light speared into the house.

And there, at the top of the long, steep staircase, stood Mrs. Hathaway.

The lightning faded. Now all Amy could see was the pale cloth of Mrs. Hathaway's nightgown.

"Mrs. Hathaway!" Amy called.

The woman did not answer. Another bolt of lightning lit the staircase.

Mrs. Hathaway's eyes were blank and empty. Unseeing as a sleepwalker's.

She took a step closer to the edge of the staircase.

The room went dim again.

"Mrs. Hathaway!" Amy screamed. "Claire!"

Amy ran toward the stairs. Her legs moved with

a strange, dreamlike slowness. Too slow. She knew she would be too late.

Now she could make out thick shadows behind Mrs. Hathaway. They formed a wall—a wall that was pushing her forward.

Mrs. Hathaway teetered at the very edge of the staircase.

One more step—and she would fall all the way down.

Mrs. Hathaway lifted one foot. Held it poised in the air.

Rage flooded through Amy. She had not come this far only to fail!

"No!" Amy cried. She shoved her arms out in front of her as though to push the older woman back. "Stop!"

The shadows behind Mrs. Hathaway almost seemed to hesitate. She stood motionless, frozen with one foot in the air.

David walked out of the darkness behind Mrs. Hathaway, his expression hard and grim.

He reached out and grabbed his mother by the shoulder.

It is going to happen, Amy thought. *And there is nothing I can do to stop it. I cannot reach her in time.*

David is going to kill his mother.

Chapter
14

Lightning flashed again. Glinting off David's black eye patch.

His fingers dug into his mother's shoulders.

Amy tried to scream, but no sound came out.

Then David dragged his mother away from the edge of the staircase. Back to safety.

Surprise and relief raged through Amy in a wild flood. She had thought such horrible things about David! But she was wrong.

Amy felt as though all her bones had melted. She sank to her knees, completely drained.

"Mother," David called. When she did not respond, he shook her gently. "Mother!"

Mrs. Hathaway gave a start. Awareness came

rushing into her face. "What happened?" she gasped. "How did I get here?"

"You were sleepwalking," David explained. His face looked pale in the flickering light of the storm. "If I had not heard Amy calling you . . ." Suddenly, fiercely, he hugged his mother.

Tears flooded Amy's eyes. She had never before seen such raw emotion, such love, in a man's face. And she knew, as surely as she knew her own name, that David could not have killed Chantal or any woman.

Amy did not want to cry. Once she started, she might not be able to stop. She pressed the heels of her hands against her eyes to hold the tears in.

She had been confused—but no more. She would never, ever doubt David again.

"You . . . you said Amy called me?" Mrs. Hathaway asked. "Is she here?"

Gently, David turned her around. Her eyes widened as she saw Amy kneeling on the floor below.

"If I had not heard Amy cry out, you would have fallen and broken your neck."

"How did she know . . . ?" Mrs. Hathaway's voice trailed away.

"I would like the answer to that as well," David replied.

He led his mother downstairs. Then he bent down and helped Amy to her feet.

Gently, he grasped Amy's chin and tilted her face up. "How did this happen?" he asked.

She glanced away, sure that David would find her

repulsive if he knew the truth. But she had to tell him. She took a deep breath.

"When I came to stay with my cousin Angelica, she showed me a strange deck of cards. She told me that she had the power to use the cards to read the future. And she said I also had the power—if I wanted it."

David and his mother stared at Amy for what seemed like a lifetime. *What are they thinking?* she wondered. *Do they think such power only comes from evil? What can they think of me?*

"Did you learn to use the cards?" David asked.

"Yes, but not like Angelica. She knows the meaning of each card, and the combinations of cards. But the cards . . . call to me. They tell me things."

"What things?" Mrs. Hathaway demanded.

She sounded frightened. Amy did not blame her. The strange power still scared *her*.

"They showed me that three people would die, and they did," Amy replied.

David drew his breath in sharply. "Nellie, Bernice, and Chantal."

Amy heard Mrs. Hathaway whimper low in her throat.

"How did you know to come here tonight?" David asked. He rubbed his hand back and forth over his good eye.

Amy rushed on. "I knew something awful was going to happen to you tonight, Mrs. Hathaway. The cards gave me a vision. So I ran over as fast as I could. But I would have been too late. If David had not been here . . ."

She could not finish the sentence. The memory was still too real, too raw.

"I am afraid," Amy whispered. A wave of cold swept through her. "From the moment I came here, I have been surrounded by death. I have watched people die—over and over and over. It is as if I am the center of a storm. I cannot stop it, I cannot get away, and it will go on and on—" Amy broke off. If she said another word she would burst into tears.

"No," David growled. "It will stop now. You are not going back to that house."

"David is right," Mrs. Hathaway agreed. "You will stay here with us, where it is safe."

They did not hate her! They did not think she was evil. Tears stung the back of Amy's eyelids.

She only wished she could believe them about being safe. More than anything, she wanted to feel safe.

"I have to go back," she told them.

Shock widened David's good eye. "You cannot!" he protested. "I will not allow you to put yourself in danger."

"But I am not in danger," she pointed out. "I am only afraid—afraid of what I will have to see next."

"What about Angelica?" David interrupted. "There are many rumors about her ability to perform dark magic. Could she be responsible for the deaths?"

Amy wrapped her arms around herself to keep from shivering. "Yes," she answered. How could she ever have believed David was the killer?

"Then why are you going back?" David demanded.

"I am family," Amy replied. "She would never hurt me. But no one else is safe—including you and your mother if you try to help me."

Mrs. Hathaway's eyes widened. "You mean—"

"If I stay here with you, she will know I turned against her," Amy explained. "And she will come after me. You will both be in terrible danger."

"Do not worry about that. I—" David began.

"No," Amy begged. "You do not understand her power."

"What do you suggest?" Mrs. Hathaway asked.

"My parents will surely send for me soon. I think Angelica will let me go to them without a struggle. So all I have to do is wait until that happens. I will pretend nothing unusual has happened, and I will be very, very careful."

"I do not like it," David growled.

"But there is no other way," Amy pointed out. "You saw what happened here tonight. You saw what she can do. I have to go back."

"She is right, David." Mrs. Hathaway's voice shook. "But Amy, you must promise you will let us know at once if you are in danger."

"I will," Amy promised.

"Let me take you home," David said. Reluctantly, he wrapped one of his mother's cloaks around Amy's wet shoulders. Then he led her out into the garden. Rain still splattered down, but the storm had moved off to the south.

As soon as they were out of sight of the house, David pulled Amy to a stop.

"Amy . . ." He hesitated for a moment, then took a deep breath. "I must tell you something. I am in love with you."

She stared at him. "What?"

"I think I knew it from the first time I met you. But I was afraid. I thought you would turn away from me because of this." He touched his patch.

"That is the silliest thing I ever heard," she said. "I told you it didn't bother me—and you know I always speak my mind."

David grinned. Amy flung her arms around his neck. "I love you, too."

He kissed her. She held on tight, wishing she never had to let him go. But finally, she stepped back.

"The night Bernice died . . ." she paused, staring into his face. "You told me never to trust you. Why?"

His smile faded. "In the war, I made friends with a boy from South Carolina. He said he was sixteen, but I knew he could not be older than fourteen. His father died in the fighting. He left his mother and five sisters alone to take his father's place. I swore to myself that I would protect him. He trusted me."

With a sigh, David raked his hand through his hair. "I failed him. He was killed, and I could not do a thing to stop it. I never wanted to feel that pain again. So I made myself a different promise. I vowed never to be responsible for another person."

David stared down at Amy. "And then you came along," he continued. "I did everything I could to leave you alone. But I could not. I want you to trust me. And I want you to depend on me to keep you safe."

"I do trust you," she murmured.

He let his breath out in a harsh sigh. Then he reached up and pulled something shiny from beneath his shirt. "I want you to have this," he said, setting it in her hand.

It was a gold ring with loops of delicate ivy etched across it. It hung on a delicate chain.

"It is beautiful," Amy murmured.

"It belonged to my grandmother, and her mother before her," David told her. His hand closed over hers, locking the ring in her palm.

Tears stung Amy's eyes. "Oh, David." She slipped the chain over her head and tucked the ring beneath her dress. It felt perfect there, just beside her heart.

"I should get you home," David said. "Before I change my mind about letting you go at all."

They did not talk as they walked toward the Fear mansion. They did not need to. Amy lifted her face into the cool breeze the storm had left behind. Her heart felt too big for her chest. David loved her!

The house loomed over them in the darkness. Amy wished she could turn and run, and never go inside it again.

"There is still time to change your mind," David whispered. "All you have to do is tell me, and we will leave."

Before Amy could say anything, the door swung open.

Light poured out, pinning them in its brightness.

Angelica stared at them from the doorway.

Chapter
15

Angelica's eyes appeared as cold and hard as ice.

"I did not know you were out, Amy," she said softly.

David stepped forward. "She was with us, Mrs. Fear."

"Indeed," Angelica replied. "Well, thank you for bringing her back, David. I will take care of her now."

Before he could say anything more, Amy hurried into the house. She turned back just as Angelica closed the door. Closing Amy in. Closing David out.

Amy swallowed hard, expecting a confrontation.

But Angelica merely stared at her for a long moment. Then she pointed toward the stairs.

Amy did not dare say anything. Grateful for the chance to escape, she ran upstairs to her room.

Amy awakened with a start. Someone was outside her bedroom door.

The doorknob turned. The door creaked open.

Amy peered into the darkness.

Julia. It was just Julia standing in the doorway. Amy's heartbeat slowed back down.

Julia glanced nervously over her shoulder, as if to make sure no one was watching. Then she scurried inside and shut the door behind her.

"Is something wrong?" Amy asked.

Julia put her finger to her lips and shook her head. She took a battered, charred piece of paper from the pocket of her dressing gown and held it out to Amy.

"Take this," she whispered. "I found it on the ash pile behind the house. Do not tell anyone I gave it to you. Promise!"

"I promise," Amy vowed. "But—"

Julia spun around and ran out of the room.

Amy stared after her for a moment. Then she closed her door and started smoothing out the wrinkled paper.

Her breath caught. This was her mother's handwriting!

Amy realized someone had tried to burn a letter to her from her mother. The paper rattled as her hands began to shake. Not in fear. In anger. Who had done this?

Angelica, of course. Angelica did not want her in communication with her parents. Angelica wanted to have complete control over Amy.

Especially now that she suspects I know the truth about her, Amy thought. How much did Angelica know? Did the cards tell Angelica that Amy had turned against her?

All you can do is be careful and try to act the same way you always have, Amy told herself.

She lit the lamp and held the paper close to the light. "Your father's recovery is slow but steady," her mother had written. The next few paragraphs were too scorched to read. Amy made a low sound of frustration.

"Your father will not be able to leave Richmond for a while," Amy read aloud.

She held the letter to her chest, triumph rushing through her. *They are in Richmond! David will be able to find them now. I can write to them, and tell them to make Angelica send me home!*

Amy found paper, pen, and ink, and sat down at the table to write. When she finished the letter, she sealed it and wrote her parents' names and Richmond, Virginia on the outside.

Now all she had to do was get the letter to David. She parted the curtains a crack and peered toward the Hathaway mansion. A light burned in an upstairs window. Good. Someone must still be up. She could slip out of the house and be back before Angelica missed her.

A tiny movement caught Amy's attention. She leaned forward. David stood on the other side of the garden gate, half hidden in the shadows.

Amy smiled. He was watching the house. Guarding her.

Her smile faded as she saw him start to turn away. "Do not go!" she whispered. "Oh, David, do not go yet!"

Amy snatched the lamp off the table. Maybe she could signal him somehow . . .

A sudden gust of wind shook the window. A tree branch clawed at the glass.

A familiar feeling of dread rippled along Amy's spine. Something was wrong. Very wrong. She could feel it.

A beam of light speared out from the open back door of the Fear house. David had returned to the gate. The wind ruffled his hair and tugged at his jacket.

As Amy peered down, a shadow fell across the light. Amy opened the window as quietly as possible. She leaned out and spotted Angelica in the doorway.

Angelica crossed the garden—heading straight toward David. What was she doing?

Angelica stopped at the garden gate. Amy watched David for any reaction. But he was too far away to read the expression on his face.

What are they talking about? Amy wondered. She would give anything to know.

Angelica and David continued to speak, their

heads close together. Then David swung on his heel and walked away.

Angelica watched him go. When she turned back to the house, her teeth gleamed in a smile.

Something bad was going to happen. Amy knew it. The air felt charged, as if a storm hovered right above the house. Amy did not like this. She did not like it at all.

Slowly, Angelica raised her arms. The wind swirled around her. Leaves and shredded flowers whirled above the ground.

The wind grew stronger and wilder, howling like a rabid wolf. The trees groaned as their branches bent.

Angelica stood at the very center of the whirlwind—untouched. Only her hair moved, lifting in a veil of darkness around her head.

Amy wanted to run. She wanted to bury her head beneath her pillows and pretend this was not happening.

But she had to watch. She had to know.

The weeping willows almost seemed to writhe in pain. Their branches lashed the fish pond into a froth.

And there, in the deepest, darkest place beneath the willows, something began to glow. Two tiny balls of green fire.

The balls moved to the edge of the willow. Amy swallowed hard, but her mouth stayed dry.

Eyes. They are eyes, she thought.

An animal's eyes can catch the light like that, she told herself.

But she knew it was no animal in the garden. Those eyes belonged to something . . . unnatural.

Amy felt very glad David had gone home. And very glad she had not gone outside to give him the letter.

The air flowing into Amy's room turned colder. And she knew why. Angelica was using her dark powers. What did her cousin have planned?

Angelica bowed to the glowing green eyes.

Amy watched Angelica reach into her pockets. Then she raised her hands overhead again—a square of white cloth in each fist. The wind tore at the squares, whipping them like tiny banners.

Dark splotches marred both cloths.

Blood.

Nellie's blood.

Chantal's blood.

What was Angelica asking for tonight? Another death?

Amy shivered. She had underestimated Angelica.

It would not matter to Angelica that Amy was part of her own family. If Angelica found out the truth about Amy, she would kill her.

Because Angelica was evil. Pure evil.

Chapter
16

Angelica dropped her arms. The wind died.

"Evil," Amy whispered.

Amy watched Angelica walk back into the house and shut the door behind her.

Then Amy noticed something that sent a shiver running through her.

The glowing green eyes remained in the garden.

They glared out from beneath the willow trees, then they began to move. Appearing and disappearing. They slid from one pocket of shadows to another.

Amy could not see the creature itself. She caught glimpses of something big and black, so black that it might have been made of shadows. She was glad that she could not see anything more.

The green eyes slid along the base of the garden wall. Then they moved back the other way. Almost, Amy thought, as if the creature were pacing back and forth.

It is standing guard, Amy realized. *Angelica summoned that creature to keep me on this side of the garden gate.*

Now she could not go to David.

And Amy hoped with all her heart he would not try to come to her.

She did not want to think about what that—that *thing*—would do to him.

Amy sat at the window and waited for the night to end. It took forever. But finally, the shadows in the garden grew thin. And the glowing green eyes dimmed.

Amy watched as the edge of the sun appeared on the horizon. Light poured over the city, flooding into the garden.

The eyes blinked out. A thin coil of smoke oozed from beneath the willows.

Amy shuddered. Then she saw movement in the Hathaways' garden. Her heartbeat quickened as she caught a glimpse of David.

This might be her only chance to give him the letter. Angelica was surely asleep, and the servants would not be up for a few more minutes. She might just have time to get to the Hathaways' and back without being discovered.

Amy slipped through the quiet house and ran

outside. Flowers lay broken on the ground, and leaves and twigs littered the path.

A flash of white on one of the willow trees caught Amy's attention. She went to investigate—and found three parallel slashes through the bark. They looked like claw marks.

Amy's nostrils flared. A nasty smell lingered there. She could not quite recognize it.

Frowning, Amy took a step away from the tree. The tree would die. She did not know how she knew, but she did. It was touched by evil, and it would die.

"Amy!" David whispered.

She whirled around. He stood at the other side of the garden gate. Concern darkened his expression.

"I am so glad to see you!" she called softly.

She ran to him. But when she tried to open the gate, she found it locked. Her gaze rose to David's.

"Angelica locked it last night," he told her. "She said I would never set foot in her garden again. And that I would never see you."

"She cannot stop us from being together." Amy reached through the iron bars, and David grabbed one of her hands.

"I know. Kiss me," David said.

Amy pressed her face against the bars. Her lips could barely brush his.

David gave the bars a fierce yank. "I would like to tear this down," he growled. "She locked it right in front of my face, and then she laughed."

Amy reached into her pocket and took out the letter. She had to get back inside. "I discovered that my parents are in Richmond," she told him. "Do you think you can find them?"

"I'll try. It will be easier now that I know what city they are in," he replied. "But Amy, we cannot wait until your parents send for you. You should leave now."

"You know I cannot," she protested. "And you know why. It is too dangerous. You have no idea how powerful Angelica is."

Amy glanced over her shoulder at the house. The servants would be moving about now. She could not chance being caught. Not this morning. "I need to get back before someone sees us," she whispered.

She started to turn away. But David would not let go of her hand.

"I must see you again," he said. "Meet me here tonight."

"No! Not at night!" Amy heard her voice tremble. "Promise me you will never come here at night!"

"Why?" he demanded. "She cannot watch us every moment."

"Promise me!" she hissed.

"But I do not understand—"

"David, you asked me to trust you, and I did," she said. "Now I am asking you to trust me. Please, please do not try to come here after dark."

He stared at her for a moment. Then he nodded. "I promise. But when will we be able to meet?"

"Watch for me. I will try to come out before it gets dark. But if I cannot, I will be here this time tomorrow morning." Amy pulled away from him.

"I love you," he said.

She blew him a kiss, then turned and hurried back to the house. She heard someone coming down the back stairway, so Amy slipped around to the front of the house. She crept inside and quietly closed the door behind her.

"Amy."

Angelica's call came from the parlor. Amy wanted to run. Instead, she walked into the room, trying to appear calm.

Angelica sat on the sofa, sewing. Just like a thousand other women in the city, Amy thought. But Angelica was unlike any of them.

"Good morning, Angelica," Amy murmured.

Angelica looked up and smiled coolly. "You are up early, my dear."

"I am always up early," Amy replied.

Angelica inclined her head. "True. Come closer, Amy."

Amy obeyed. She had no choice.

Angelica looked so beautiful in the morning sunlight. Her eyes were bright, her hair shiny. Her skin was glowing with health.

"You look well this morning, Angelica," Amy said.

"Thank you," Angelica replied. "It must be because I am so excited about tonight's celebration."

"Celebration?" Amy asked.

"It is All Hallows' Eve, dear. We are going to have a party tonight," Angelica explained. "I was wondering if you would help me decorate the house today. Your mother told me that you have a talent for such things."

"Of course," Amy replied. How much did Angelica know? Did she think Amy was sneaking out simply to see David? Or did she realize that Amy had discovered the truth? The truth that Angelica was a murderer.

"Oh, good!" Angelica exclaimed. "I love All Hallows' Eve. I think it is the best holiday of the year."

"Better than Christmas?" Amy asked. She wanted to appear interested in the celebration—to keep Angelica off guard.

"Oh, yes." Angelica laughed. "We are going to have so much fun!"

At least there will be lots of people around, Amy told herself. Although that did not help poor Bernice. She pushed that thought away.

"What would you like me to do first, Angelica?" Amy asked.

"I want every vase in the house filled with flowers, and perhaps some fall leaves and berries," Angelica said.

"When the girls come downstairs, they might like to help me," Amy said. "I enjoyed such things when I was their age."

"Oh, the children are spending the day with some friends," Angelica replied. "One of the servants is driving them. They left before dawn because it is such a long trip. But they will return in time for our party."

She is lying, Amy thought. She wanted the children out of the house for some reason.

Amy suddenly realized how still the house was. Where were the servants? Were they gone too?

"Is the cook preparing something special?" Amy asked.

Angelica shook her head. "I decided to give all the servants the day off. Now they will be able to enjoy the holiday too."

Angelica wanted the house empty. Why? What does she have planned?

The cards, Amy thought. The cards would tell her. If she learned what Angelica was planning, she would have an advantage.

But Angelica would not let Amy out of her sight. They gathered greenery from the garden together. They ate their noon meal together. They worked on all the flower arrangements together.

Amy grew more and more anxious as it got later and later. *It will be dark soon,* she thought. I need to know Angelica's plans now.

Amy glanced over at Angelica. She was absorbed in arranging greens on the mantel. Amy picked up a vase and deliberately spilled water all over her dress.

"Ohh!" Amy gasped. "I am so clumsy. I'll just run upstairs and change my clothes."

"Very well," Angelica answered, sounding annoyed.

Amy dashed up to the third floor. If she was gone too long Angelica would become suspicious.

The air in Angelica's study felt thick and smelled musty, as if the room had been shut up for years. But the moment Amy touched the cards, her awareness of everything else faded.

"Angelica is not the only one with power," she

murmured. Her hands began to itch and burn, and Amy began to shuffle the deck.

The cards seemed to be in a hurry, as though they needed to tell her something that could not wait. *What is Angelica planning?* Amy thought.

Amy cut the deck into three piles, then stacked them together, right to left. The cards felt hot. Her hands started to shake.

"What is it?" she whispered. She set the cards down and turned over the top one.

Death.

She shuddered. Of course. Death followed her everywhere.

Her breath rasped in her ears as she turned the next card over.

Death.

No. Amy stared down at the two identical cards. It is not possible, she thought. There is only one Death card in the tarot.

Gingerly, she reached out and flipped over the entire deck. Cards slithered across the polished wood of the desk.

Amy let out a sound that was part gasp, part sob.

Death.

Every card Death.

Chapter
17

"No!" Amy cried. "I don't understand what you are trying to tell me. I must know more. I have to know who will die!"

She picked up the cards but they were cool and lifeless in her hands. There was nothing more to learn from them.

And then Amy realized what the cards were trying to tell her. Angelica's next victim would be *Amy*. That was why every card was Death.

Stay calm, Amy ordered herself. Try to stay calm. Remember what happened to Mrs. Hathaway. The cards showed she would be the next to die. But you and David were able to save her.

Amy had to return to Angelica before her cousin became suspicious. Then she had to find a way to escape. Oh, why couldn't the cards have told her more?

Amy quietly slipped out of Angelica's study and shut the door behind her. As she scurried down the hall, she stepped on something hard. Something that cut through the thin sole of her shoe.

Amy leaned against the wall and pulled the sharp object out of her foot. What is it? she wondered. She turned it over in her hands.

Bone, she realized. It is a piece of bone!

Amy shuddered and threw the bone down. She again heard Julia's warning: It ate him—flesh and bone and blood. Was the evil creature Julia had seen that night loose in the house again?

Amy raced down to the second floor. Her hurt foot throbbed as she rushed along the hall to the main staircase. She ignored the pain.

She grabbed the banister, ready to dash down the curving staircase. But the banister felt slick. Amy raised her hand and stared at her palm. It was covered with blood.

Flesh and bone and blood. The words echoed through Amy's mind. It ate him *flesh and bone and blood.*

Amy swallowed hard. She plunged down the marble steps, taking them two and three at a time.

Better to break her neck, she thought, than to let that evil thing have her.

She jumped down the last few steps. Gasping, she dashed to the front door.

Locked. "No!" She panted, tearing at the knob with all her strength. "Oh, no!"

"You are not thinking of leaving before our party begins, are you?" Amy whirled around. Angelica stood watching her.

"What evil have you brought into this house? What have you done?" Amy cried.

"Only what you have forced me to do," Angelica replied.

Amy could not make her voice work. She could only stare as Angelica closed her eyes and raised her hands over her head—just as she had in the garden.

A breeze swirled through the room, setting the chandelier in motion. When Angelica opened her eyes again, Amy's knees buckled.

Angelica's eyes were no longer green. They were black. Pure black.

The panels of the door dug into Amy's back as she pressed herself against it. "It cannot be!" she moaned.

"Ah, but it can," Angelica said. The black pits of her eyes glistened. There was no mercy in those eyes, no softness in the lovely, sculpted lines of her face.

She was cold. Pitiless. Evil.

"I told you that All Hallows' Eve was my favorite holiday," Angelica said. "As it is for my guests. They expect a special treat on that day, and I always give them one."

She smiled. Her teeth seemed longer than usual, so bright and sharp. "Tonight," she continued, staring straight at Amy, "I will give them . . . you."

Chapter
18

Angelica gestured to the top of the staircase. Amy's gaze shot up—and she stifled a scream.

A column of thick black smoke stretched from the top stair to the ceiling.

She is going to give me to that hideous thing!

"That column holds my spirits, my friends, my guides. Some of them have been with me since I was very young. Once, I was like you. Frightened of the power inside me. But not anymore."

She is so cold, so calm, Amy thought. *She is chatting with me as if we are at a party together. And she is planning to kill me!*

"I am very disappointed in you," Angelica told Amy, a slight frown marring her beautiful face.

"W-why?" Amy stuttered. *Keep the conversa-*

tion going, she told herself. It would give her more time to find a way to escape.

"I was so looking forward to having another powerful Pierce woman in the family," Angelica explained. "We could have done so much together. You have missed an incredible opportunity by turning against me."

"To be evil?" she asked. Amy knew the door behind her was locked. And if she tried to run past Angelica, the spirits could swoop down on her.

"There is great power in evil," Angelica replied. "Oh, Amy. You could have had anything you wanted."

Amy nodded, pretending she was listening hard to every word.

Angelica smiled. "Well, anything but David," she added. "I am saving him for Hannah."

"Hannah!" Amy cried, her full attention now on her cousin.

"When she gets older, of course," Angelica said. "They are perfect for each other."

"How can you say that?" Amy demanded.

"The Hathaways are very wealthy," Angelica told her. "David will marry Hannah and bring that fortune to the Fears."

"Even if you kill me, David would never marry Hannah," Amy protested.

"David will have no say about it. I can easily control him," Angelica answered. "He will marry Hannah, and I will make sure he does exactly what I want him to do."

"It will never work." Amy knew David better

than Angelica did. She knew how strong he truly was. How much death he had seen and survived.

Angelica stared at Amy with her black eyes—and Amy felt pain shoot through her brain. "Oh yes, Amy. David will do what I tell him."

Angelica leaned close. Amy felt waves of coldness coming off her cousin's body. "You have great potential. But you lack the courage to use it. When my spirits finish with you, your power will belong to me."

"I know you killed them all," Amy whispered. "Nellie, Bernice, Chantal—"

"Of course," Angelica replied. "Death pleases my spirits. And it adds to my power."

She reached out and ran her fingertip along Amy's cheek. Amy had to clench her fists to keep from pulling away from that cold touch.

"Is it such a surprise, my dear?" Angelica asked. "I killed Chantal because you would not listen to me. You kept finding ways to see David. So I had my spirits kill Chantal and give you that vision. Most people would have run screaming from David. But not you. You are too stubborn."

Angelica glanced behind her at the column of black smoke waiting at the top of the stairs. "Perhaps it is just as well. Now my spirits can feast on you. They will enjoy you. And then I will have your power for my own."

Angelica half-turned, and Amy knew her one chance had come. She darted to the right, heading toward the back of the house.

But Angelica was too quick. Much too quick. She

grabbed Amy's arm in a grip that numbed it to the elbow.

Amy struggled, kicking and scratching, as her cousin pulled her to the stairs.

"Foolish girl," Angelica taunted. "It is too late for you. Much too late."

When they neared the top of the stairs, the pillar moved away from them. Angelica followed it up to her study, pulling Amy behind her.

Amy's breath came in ragged pants. "Angelica, do not do this. What . . . what will you tell my parents?"

"I will tell them you fell ill," Angelica replied. She forced Amy into the study and shut the door behind them. "Or I will tell them you had an accident. Such things happen to people frequently."

Amy could feel the hunger inside the oily black pillar. She knew how much it wanted her.

Her feet skidded across the smooth wood floor as Angelica pulled her closer to the oily column. "Oh, please, no!"

Angelica flung Amy onto the floor in front of the twisting column. Cold poured from it in waves. Amy felt her body slow down and begin to freeze.

The stink of rotting flesh filled her mouth, gagging her. She could taste it on her tongue, in her throat.

Tendrils of black smoke oozed toward Amy. They slid back and forth along the floor like horrible, blind worms.

It was coming for her.

Chapter
19

It wanted blood. And not just any blood. Her blood.

Flesh and bone and blood.

"Take her!" Angelica cried in triumph.

A screech of terror escaped Amy.

"That's right, Amy," Angelica said, her voice cool and calm. "Scream. The spirits enjoy that. It will make the end that much sweeter for them."

The black pillar swept down on Amy. Covering her completely.

Amy curled up in a tight little ball. She squeezed her eyes shut.

"Aaa-mmmm-yyy . . ." a voice called. *"Aaa-mmmm-yyy."*

A woman's voice. But not her cousin's.

"Aaa-mmm-yyy."

Amy opened her eyes. All she could see was the black smoke. It was thick and oily. It left a greasy film on her hands and face. What was happening to her?

"Aaa-mmmm-yyy."

A face appeared in the smoke. A face covered with sores. Raw, bone-deep sores that oozed yellow pus.

A sharp, bitter taste hit the back of Amy's throat. She swallowed hard.

More faces appeared around Amy. "No," Amy moaned. "Please. I can't bear it."

One face was wet with blood. Its eyeballs hung by threads.

One face had a ragged hole in its forehead. Amy could see a clump of spongy brain tissue inside.

Another had been skinned, leaving a flayed, bloody mask covered with spidery blue veins.

Still another face was so bloated that it hardly looked human at all. It opened its mouth to scream, and a white, squirming horde of maggots crawled out.

I know her, Amy thought, horrified. I know that woman.

It was the face of Chantal Duvane.

With a shock, Amy realized what the faces were. *Who* they were.

They were the faces of all the people Angelica had killed.

If Angelica won, Amy would be held prisoner in the twisting column too.

Amy screamed, screamed until she had to gasp for breath.

"You brought this on yourself, Amy dear," Amy heard Angelica call.

"How could you?" Amy shouted. "How could you do this to me?"

"But, Amy, I can do anything!" Angelica answered.

The faces crowded close to Amy, moaning and screeching. Their eyes stared into hers. They licked her with their decaying tongues.

Then clawed hands appeared in the black smoke. They reached for Amy.

She forced herself to her feet and whirled one way, then the other. Avoiding the worst of the slashes.

"That's it," Angelica called. Her voice sounded so far away. "Fight, Amy. Or maybe you should beg. They like their victims to beg."

The claws tore at Amy's hair. Her dress. They raked painfully across her arms.

They could kill me so easily, Amy realized. They are playing with me. Torturing me for pleasure.

Or they wanted more from her than her life.

Yes! That was it. They wanted more than her body. They wanted her soul.

If they took it, she would be trapped in the pillar with the others. Howling and screaming. Reliving her death again and again.

"Nooooo!" she shrieked.

The oily black smoke lifted her off her feet and held her suspended in the air.

Amy expected pain. But she only felt cold. So cold.

Close your eyes, Amy. The voice slid through her mind. Smooth and soft and inhuman. So different from the voices howling in agony around her.

This is not the voice of one of her victims, Amy thought. It must be one of her guides. It is evil, Amy told herself. You cannot listen to it.

Close your eyes, and it will all be over.

The voice tugged at Amy. She struggled to remember why she should not obey. Her eyelids quivered and began to close.

It is the end, she thought. The end of everything. She would slide into darkness, and the fear would stop forever. It would be so easy . . .

And then Amy heard Angelica laughing. Laughing.

Anger washed through her, burning away the paralyzing cold. She was not going to give up. She could not. Her parents needed her. David needed her. And she was not about to let Angelica win.

Slowly, Amy forced her eyes open. Something new burst to life within her, something deep and powerful. Sparks blossomed in front of her eyes and liquid fire ran through her body.

Close your eyes, Amy, and it will all be over.

"No!" Amy shouted. She felt strong. So strong.

This is what Angelica wanted to steal from me, Amy realized. This power. My *power.*

"You cannot have it," Amy screamed. She fought against the blackness surrounding her.

The faces pressed close to Amy, as though afraid

they might lose her. Their stench poured into her nose and mouth, suffocating her.

No, she thought. *No!*

Amy's power burned through her, growing hotter and hotter. Stronger and stronger.

Then it exploded outward in a flash of light.

For a moment, Amy was blinded. Then she saw the oily black smoke shriveling away like burning hair.

Amy dropped to the floor. Free! She was free!

Then she looked down at herself—and gasped.

Tiny white flames flickered along her skin. Bright, so bright they hurt her eyes. But they did not burn her.

Amy caught something moving from the corner of her eye. The oily pillar. As she watched, it began to whirl faster and faster.

The faces stared at Amy, howling in fury.

"Stop," she whispered. But they did not. The howl went up and up, louder and louder.

Pain shot through Amy. "Stop!" she yelled.

Balls of white fire flew off her body and into the pillar.

A crack appeared in the dark column. It spread and widened.

Then the whole mass split apart. The faces tearing. Screaming in agony.

A mixture of blood and an oily black liquid spattered across the room.

Then the horrible howling stopped.

Amy could not stop shaking. It's over, she told herself. It's over.

But what about Angelica? Amy spun around.

Her cousin lay on the floor, arms and legs sprawled awkwardly. Her hair spread in a black pool around her.

Did I kill her? Amy wondered. Did destroying Angelica's spirits kill her?

Chapter
20

—————

"What have you done?" Angelica cried weakly.

She wasn't dead! "Your spirits are gone," Amy told her cousin.

"No! It can't be true!"

"But it is," Amy said firmly. "It's over, Angelica. You failed. You could use your spirits to kill Chantal and Bernice. And poor Nellie. They could not fight you. But I can. And I won."

Amy stared down at Angelica. She noticed that her cousin's eyes had turned green again.

"Good-bye, Angelica," Amy said softly. Then she rushed from the room.

"You cannot get away!" Angelica screamed as Amy pounded down the stairs.

Her voice spurred Amy to go faster. She had to get out now. Angelica could regain her strength at any moment.

She had to get to David. She had to warn him!

She ran to the front door.

Locked.

Amy had forgotten it was locked. Maybe the housekeeper kept a set in the kitchen or pantry. She hurried into the kitchen and searched through the drawers and cupboards as quickly as she could.

Where are they? Where are they?

Amy didn't know what Angelica would do to her if she came downstairs. She knew the column of spirits had been destroyed. She *felt* it. But that did not mean Angelica had no other powers.

Amy crossed over to the pantry door. As she opened it, she heard something jingle. An apron hung on the doorknob. And in the apron pocket—the keys!

She ran to the front door. She tried three keys—then found one that worked.

Then she rushed toward the Hathaways' home. At the gate, she tried one key after another. Did the housekeeper have the gate key on her ring?

Amy's hands shook as she tried another key.

She heard a twig crack behind her.

Angelica was coming. Or something else. Something worse.

"Please," she whispered, frantically fitting another key into the lock. She twisted it back and forth. "Come on, come on!"

The lock clicked. Amy shoved the gate open and dashed toward the Hathaway mansion.

She could see a light through the mist. Good. Someone was home.

A dark shape appeared in front of Amy. She did not have time to stop. Her breath went out in a grunt as she crashed into it.

A strong arm came around her and kept her from falling. Amy jerked her head up. "David!" she exclaimed. "Hurry, we have to get back to your house. We are in terrible danger. Angelica is going to—"

Her words ended in a gasp as he scooped her up with his good arm. "You do not need to carry me, David. I'm fine. Really. And we will be able to go faster if we both run."

He did not listen. His arm tightened around her, squeezing her ribs painfully.

Amy stared at him in rising horror. "David," she cried. "What's wrong?"

He did not answer.

He started walking.

Walking straight toward the Fear mansion.

He was taking her back to Angelica!

Chapter
21

"No," Amy moaned. "Oh, please, not this!"

David did not answer her. He did not even glance down at her. He just kept walking—walking toward the Fear mansion.

Amy struggled to slide out of his grasp, but his arm felt like iron around her waist.

"David, it is me—Amy," she cried. "Can't you hear me?"

She grabbed his face and forced him to look at her.

There was no recognition in his face. No expression at all.

Angelica did this, Amy thought. Angelica is controlling him.

Now even David could not help her.

Amy felt tears run down her face. She had barely escaped from Angelica the first time. What could she do against her cousin now?

Amy shook her head. "No. Angelica cannot have you, David. I will fight for you—and myself. And I will beat her."

Amy pounded against David's chest with her fists, determined to force him to hear her. "David, it's Amy. You told me you love me. And I love you. Oh, please remember, David!"

He ignored her. His long strides jolted her as he carried her toward the Fear mansion.

Amy had to find a way to reach him. If she didn't, Angelica would destroy them both.

David had almost reached the back door.

Angelica knew this was the way to hurt her the most. Anger burned inside Amy. I will not let her take David. I will never let him marry Hannah.

"David, listen to me," Amy ordered, her voice sharp. "You have to fight. Do not let her tell you what to do. Fight!"

David carried her into the house and set Amy down. He kept a tight hold on her arm.

Amy tried to pull his fingers off her. But David would not release her.

"Welcome back, Amy," Angelica said. She walked toward them, regal as a queen.

"Let him go," Amy demanded.

"Ah, but he is mine," Angelica replied, smiling. "Let me show you."

She crooked her finger at him. "David, bring her to me."

"No, David," Amy cried. "Don't! You told me to trust you and I do. You cannot give me to her."

David hesitated.

I knew he could hear me! Amy thought. I knew he could hear me somehow.

Then David stepped forward, still clenching her arm. Her shoes scraped on the floor as he dragged her forward.

"Now it is over," Angelica said.

Amy locked her eyes on David's face. Angelica might have missed that brief hesitation, but Amy had not.

David was fighting. Inside he was struggling as hard as she was.

"Your precious David belongs to me," Angelica continued. "For as long as he amuses Hannah, that is. When she tires of him, I will add him to my little menagerie."

Amy saw something flicker in David's good eye. A flash of awareness. If Amy could reach him, if she could break him free of Angelica's control, they might have a chance.

She twisted around so that she stood in front of David. As she turned, her ring slipped outside her dress.

The ring on the gold chain David had given her. The symbol of their love for each other.

Amy threw her arms around him. She concentrated every thought on him. Every feeling. Calling to him in every way she knew how.

Her power surged deep inside her. Then it sprang free and raged like wildfire through her veins.

"David," she begged. "Look at me."

He started to glance down.

"David," Angelica snapped. "You will look only at me. You will hear only my voice."

His face stiffened into a blank mask again. His gaze fastened on Angelica.

"Kill her, David," Angelica commanded. "Kill Amy now!"

"No, David," Amy whispered. "Look at me. Remember who you are. Remember I love you."

She reached up her free hand and stroked his cheek. A white flame leapt to life where she touched him. It ran up her arm to her neck. Then it travelled to the gold ring.

When the flame hit the gold it blazed so brightly Amy could hardly look at it.

David blinked. He dropped Amy's arm. He backed a few steps away from her.

Then, with a smooth, deadly movement, he pulled out his revolver.

And pointed it at Amy.

Chapter
22

———

Amy stared straight into the muzzle of the gun.

She could not even scream.

It is over, she thought. She waited for the bullet to slam into her face.

Then David swung the revolver past her. Straight toward Angelica.

The world seemed to explode.

Pinwheels danced across Amy's vision, and her ears rang. But she could still hear the sound of Angelica's scream.

Amy turned and saw Angelica fall to her knees. A red stain spread across the shoulder of her gown.

"Come on!" David shouted. He hauled her outside and they ran for the garden gate.

As they ran, the garden itself had turned against them. Branches clutched at their clothes. Ivy wrapped itself around their feet.

"Angelica is still trying to stop us!" Amy yelled. "This is her dark magic."

"Hurry," David urged. "Once we are back in my garden, perhaps we will be safe."

Amy ran faster, her chest burning, her legs aching.

Then something grabbed Amy's foot. She crashed to the ground. Ivy slithered up her body.

David tore it away. But it sprouted again, growing faster than he could destroy it.

It wrapped around her neck. Pulling tighter and tighter.

Amy could not breathe.

She clawed at the ivy. Trying to dig her fingernails under it so she could rip it away.

Too tight. Too tight.

A roaring sound filled her ears.

Black spots appeared before her eyes.

Too tight . . .

Chapter
23

———

"Hang on, Amy!" David cried. "Don't give up now!"

David jerked the ivy away from her neck—just enough for her to suck in a short breath.

"No!" she screamed. She would not lose now!

"No!" she screamed again—and the ivy burst into flame.

My power, Amy thought. Mine.

A line of bright white fire spread from it.

The fire raced the length of the garden. It formed a wall protecting Amy and David from Angelica and her evil.

David lifted Amy to her feet. He supported her with his good arm as they stumbled to the gate.

The moment they crossed into David's garden, everything grew still.

Amy stopped and stared back at the Fear garden. Angelica stood on the far side of the flame barrier. No wound marked her shoulder. No blood stained her gown.

Their eyes locked. Then Amy turned away.

The carriage rolled quietly down the street.

"Are you sure we must leave home, David?" Mrs. Hathaway asked softly.

"Very sure," he replied.

Amy stared out the window. Watching the hulking Fear mansion grow smaller and smaller behind them.

She remembered the first time she saw it. Deep inside she had known there was something wrong in the house even then.

Fear. It was the perfect name for the house and the woman who lived there.

"I wish I could have said good-bye to Julia," Amy murmured.

"Julia belongs to the Fears," David said. "No one can help her."

Amy sat back in her seat. Poor Julia, she thought. At least the girl had not witnessed Amy's confrontation with Angelica. If she were lucky, she might never find out about her mother's evil.

She leaned her head back against the seat. The farther they travelled from that terrible house, the lighter her heart became.

"Let's all make a vow," Amy suggested.

"What kind?" Mrs. Hathaway asked.

"I have seen enough horrible things to last me the rest of my life," Amy replied. "And I want to leave them behind."

"I think I understand," David said.

"We will never speak the name Fear again," Amy declared.

They reached out and clasped hands, sealing the pact.

About the Author

"Where do you get your ideas?"

That's the question that R. L. Stine is asked most often. "I don't know where my ideas come from," he says. "But I do know that I have a lot more scary stories in my mind that I can't wait to write."

So far, he has written nearly five dozen mysteries and thrillers for young people, all of them bestsellers.

Bob grew up in Columbus, Ohio. Today he lives in an apartment near Central Park in New York City with his wife, Jane, and son, Matt.

The Fear family has many dark secrets.
The family curse has touched many lives.
Discover the truth about them all in the

FEAR STREET SAGAS

Next . . .
FORBIDDEN SECRETS
(Coming mid-August 1996)

Savannah Gentry is thrilled when Tyler Fier asks her
to marry him. But her sister, Victoria, warns her not
to go through with the wedding. Victoria tells Savannah that Tyler's family is cursed.

Savannah ignores her sister. She is sure Tyler will
make her happy. She insists that Victoria accompany
her to his family's mansion. But when they arrive,
Savannah begins to think she should have listened to
Victoria.

Everything in their new home is strange. The garden
is filled with black roses, the housekeeper tells Savannah she is not wanted there, and no one ever comes to
call on them.

Victoria insists that if they stay, either she or Savannah will end up dead. What should Savannah do?

WE NEED YOU

TO HELP R.L. STINE WRITE
FEAR STREET®: THE BEST FRIEND 2

When THE BEST FRIEND came out two years ago, hundreds of you wrote in to tell us how unhappy you were with the story—you wanted Honey to pay for her evildoings . . .

Now, the book YOU demanded.
Write in and tell us:
"What Should Happen to Honey?"

R.L. Stine will choose the essay he likes best and will write

FEAR STREET: THE BEST FRIEND 2
in October 1997 using ideas based on the winning story.

The winner will receive 5 copies of the book
autographed by R.L. Stine.

No purchase necessary. If you would like your entry to be considered for the "What Should Happen to Honey?" contest, please submit an essay no longer than 500 words. Please send with it your name, age, mailing address, photo and your parent's signature saying it is OK to use your name and story idea to: Pocket Books, Honey Contest 13th fl, 1230 Avenue of the Americas, New York, NY 10020. One entry per person. Signed submissions constitute permission to use all or part of story idea, name, address and photo in Fear Street: The Best Friend 2 book. Submission does not guarantee use. Incomplete submissions and submissions received after August 1, 1996 will not be considered. Not responsible for lost, damaged or misdirected mail. No materials will be returned. Void where prohibited. All entries will be judged equally on the basis of originality and consistency with the Fear Street series. In case of a tie the winner will be chosen at random from tying entries. Pocket Books and R.L. Stine reserve the right to use all or part of the winning story. All decisions of the judges are final. Winner's parent or legal guardian must execute and return an affidavit of eligibility and liability/publicity release within 15 days of notification attempt or an alternate winner will be selected. You must be a U.S. resident aged 16 or younger as of 8/1/96. Sole compensation for winning entry will be 5 copies of Fear Street: The Best Friend 2 autographed by R.L. Stine. Non-winning entries will receive no compensation. Employees of Viacom Inc. and their families are not eligible to participate.

1218